BELIEVE
Kids' Edition

SELECTIONS FROM THE
NEW INTERNATIONAL READER'S VERSION

BELIEVE
Kids' Edition

GENERAL EDITOR
RANDY FRAZEE

ZONDERVAN
Believe: Kids' Edition
Copyright © 2015 by Zondervan

Requests for information should be addressed to:
Zondervan, 3900 *Sparks Drive SE, Grand Rapids, Michigan,* 49546

ISBN: 978-0-310-74601-0

Cover and interior illustrations: Macky Pamintuan

Printed in the United States of America

15 16 17 18 19 20 21 22 23 24 25 /DCI/ 18 17 16 15 14 13 12 11 10 9 8 7 6 5 4 3 2 1

Table of Contents

Who Am I Becoming?

Preface

Imagine it: the people of Israel don't believe in God or worship him. They have forgotten him. Then they crown as king a boy named Josiah, and everything changes. Josiah was only eight years old when he became king. (They made him a special throne so his feet could reach the floor when he sat!)

Josiah may have been young, but he was wise enough to love God very much. One of the king's men read God's Word to Josiah. God's people were not living the way God wanted them to. This made Josiah so sad that he started to cry. He wanted his people to love God again. Young King Josiah gathered the people to hear God's Word as he had. The people promised to follow God again. Then Josiah burned everything in the nation that did not honor God.

Second Kings 23:25 tells us: "There was no king like Josiah either before him or after him. None of them turned to the LORD as he did. He obeyed the LORD with all his heart and all his soul. He obeyed him with all his strength." You can be a mighty leader for God, just like King Josiah. No one is too young to lead others to God. But you have to follow him with all your heart, soul and strength. And to do that, you have to know what you believe in the Bible. This book will help you with that.

Remember that *believe* is an action word. That means God doesn't want you to just believe in your head that his Word is truth; he wants you to believe it with your whole heart so that it changes how you live your life and relate to your family and friends. He wants to put the "extra" in your "ordinary" so you can live an "extraordinary" life in Christ. The possibilities are limitless with God for those who simply BELIEVE!

— Randy Frazee
General Editor

Introduction

To be read by the parent or teacher:

One of the greatest needs in a child's life is for parents, extended family, and leaders and teachers to pass on the Christian faith to them. Each child should clearly know what they believe and why. They should know how to practice their faith and have an understanding of God's vision for them. *Believe: Kids' Edition* is designed to assist you in accomplishing this heartfelt objective.

Scripture

Believe: Kids' Edition includes the actual words of the Bible. This is not one person's or one church's words on these important, life-altering topics. The Bible text alone is our source of teaching on each of these beliefs. *Believe: Kids' Edition* contains portions of Scripture that were thoughtfully and carefully excerpted from the Bible because they specifically explain the belief. Each belief is described using at least one Old Testament and one New Testament story from the Bible. The Scripture text used in *Believe: Kids' Edition* is taken from the New International Reader's Version (NIrV).

Book Sections

As you and your child read *Believe: Kids' Edition*, you will read three ten-chapter sections:

THINK. The first ten chapters are about the key Beliefs of the Christian life. Together they answer the question, "What do I believe?"

ACT. The second ten chapters discuss the key Practices of the Christian life. Together they answer the question, "What should I do?"

BE. The final ten chapters contain the key Virtues of the Christian life. Together they answer the question, "Who am I becoming?"

Chapter Features

Each chapter contains several elements to guide you through your *Believe: Kids' Edition* journey.

The Keys

Key Question

The key question is the starting place; this is what the chapter will help the reader think about.

Key Idea

The key idea puts words to the beliefs. Encourage your child to memorize the key ideas so they can recite what they believe.

Key Verse

The key verse for each belief is the most important Scripture about that subject. The 30 key verses are also important to memorize. God's Word hidden in young hearts will stick with them for a lifetime!

Think About It

The chapter opens with a Think About It section, where the belief that is about to be explored is summarized, and the reader is introduced to why this belief is so important.

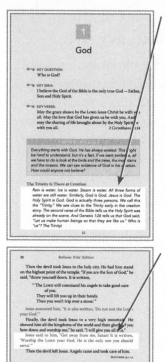

Introductions

The introductory paragraphs that set up the Scripture text appear in *italic*. They were written to guide the reader through the chapter and connect the dots between each story. The introductions have been carefully written so that they allow the Scripture to express the beliefs, rather than telling the reader what their beliefs ought to be.

Core Truths

As you read the Scripture, you will see core truths in blue. The core truth is the main point of that Scripture passage, and it helps explain why that particular passage was chosen.

Discussion Questions

There are questions at the end of each chapter to help kids explore the meaning of the Scripture and understand how each belief matters in our lives.

Tips for Enjoying Believe: Kids' Edition

To get the most out of reading this book, try these tips:

1. Read each chapter with the child. Older children may want to read independently, but be available for questions.
2. Encourage the child to ask you questions or make comments and observations about what they have read or heard.
3. Discuss the questions at the end of the chapter. Sharing thoughts with others is a great way to dig deeper.
4. Pray with the child at the end of your study time.

The *Believe* project is a comprehensive Bible engagement plan for an entire family or church. To check out all the available resources, go to www.believethestory.com for more information.

What Do I Believe?

Your heart will be where your riches are.
Matthew 6:21

What you believe in your heart matters. It sets the course for who you become. God wants you to become more like Jesus. In fact, this is who he created you to be! *Becoming* more like Jesus begins with *thinking* like Jesus.

The following ten chapters are about the key beliefs you need to believe in your heart if you want to follow Jesus. These beliefs were taught and lived by Jesus when he lived on earth. Each chapter contains two or three stories from the Bible about each belief. You will discover what God wants you to know and believe. Understanding these truths in your mind *and* heart is the first step to becoming like Jesus so that you can say, "I believe ..."

1. The God of the Bible is the only true God — Father, Son and Holy Spirit.
2. God is involved in and cares about my daily life.
3. A person can have a relationship with God by God's grace through faith in Jesus Christ.
4. The Bible is God's Word and it guides my beliefs and actions.
5. I am significant because I am a child of God.
6. God uses the church to bring about his plan.
7. All people are loved by God and need Jesus Christ as their Savior.
8. God calls all Christians to show compassion to people in need.
9. Everything I am and everything I own belong to God.
10. There is a heaven and a hell and Jesus will return to establish his eternal kingdom.

God

○━π **KEY QUESTION:**
Who is God?

○━π **KEY IDEA:**
I believe the God of the Bible is the only true God —
Father, Son and Holy Spirit.

○━π **KEY VERSE:**
May the grace shown by the Lord Jesus Christ be with you
all. May the love that God has given us be with you. And
may the sharing of life brought about by the Holy Spirit be
with you all.   *2 Corinthians 13:14*

THINK ABOUT IT

*Everything starts with God. He has always existed. This might
be hard to understand, but it's a fact. If we want evidence, all
we have to do is look at the birds and the trees, the mountains
and the oceans. We can see evidence of God in his creation.
How could anyone not believe?*

The Trinity Is There at Creation

*Rain is water. Ice is water. Steam is water. All three forms of
water are still water. Similarly, God is God. Jesus is God. The
Holy Spirit is God. God is actually three persons. We call this
the "Trinity." We see clues to the Trinity early in the creation
story. The second verse of the Bible tells us the Holy Spirit was
already on the scene. And Genesis 1:26 tells us that God said,
"Let us make human beings so that they are like us." Who is
"us"? The Trinity!*

In the beginning, God created the heavens and the earth. The earth didn't have any shape. And it was empty. There was darkness over the surface of the waves. At that time, the Spirit of God was hovering over the waters.

God said, "Let there be light." And there was light. God saw that the light was good. He separated the light from the darkness. God called the light "day." He called the darkness "night." There was evening, and there was morning. It was day one.

God said, "Let there be a huge space between the waters. Let it separate water from water." And that's exactly what happened. God made the huge space between the waters. He separated the water under the space from the water above it. God called the huge space "sky." There was evening, and there was morning. It was day two.

God said, "Let the water under the sky be gathered into one place. Let dry ground appear." And that's exactly what happened. God called the dry ground "land." He called all the water that was gathered together "seas." And God saw that it was good.

Then God said, "Let the land produce plants. Let them produce their own seeds. And let there be trees on the land that grow fruit with seeds in it. Let each kind of plant or tree have its own kind of seeds." And that's exactly what happened. So the land produced plants. Each kind of plant had its own kind of seeds. And the land produced trees that grew fruit with seeds in it. Each kind of tree had its own kind of seeds. God saw that it was good. There was evening, and there was morning. It was day three.

God said, "Let there be lights in the huge space of the sky. Let them separate the day from the night. Let the lights set the times for the holy celebrations and the days and the years. Let them be lights in the huge space of the sky to give light on the earth." And that's exactly what happened. God made two great lights. He made the larger light to rule over the day and the smaller light to rule over the night. He also made the stars. God put the lights in the huge space of the sky to give light on the earth. He put them there to rule over the day and the night. He put them there to separate light from darkness. God saw that it was good. There was evening, and there was morning. It was day four.

God said, "Let the seas be filled with living things. Let birds fly above the earth across the huge space of the sky." So God created the great sea creatures. He created every kind of living thing that fills the seas and moves about in them. He created every kind of bird that flies. And God saw that it was good. God blessed them. He said, "Have little ones so that there will be many of you. Fill the water in the seas. Let there be more and more birds on the earth." There was evening, and there was morning. It was day five.

God said, "Let the land produce every kind of living creature. Let there be livestock, and creatures that move along the ground, and wild animals." And that's exactly what happened. God made every kind of wild animal. He made every kind of livestock. He made every kind of creature that moves along the ground. And God saw that it was good.

Then God said, "Let us make human beings so that they are like us. Let them rule over the fish in the seas and the birds in the sky. Let them rule over the livestock and all the wild animals. And let them rule over all the creatures that move along the ground."

GENESIS 1:1–26

The Trinity Is There at Jesus' Baptism

We also get a glimpse of all three members of the Trinity in the New Testament at Jesus' baptism. Jesus was baptized in the Jordan River. He was baptized by his cousin John the Baptist, a great man of God. When Jesus was baptized, the Holy Spirit came to rest on him in the form of a dove, and God the Father spoke to him from heaven.

The people were waiting. They were expecting something. They were all wondering in their hearts if John might be the Messiah. John answered them all, "I baptize you with water. But one who is more powerful than I am will come. I'm not good enough to untie the straps of his sandals. He will baptize you with the Holy Spirit and fire. His pitchfork is in his hand to toss the straw away from his threshing floor. He will gather the wheat into his barn. But he will burn up the husks with fire that can't be put out." John said many other things to warn the people. He also announced the good news to them.   LUKE 3:15–18

When all the people were being baptized, Jesus was baptized too. And as he was praying, heaven was opened. The Holy Spirit came to rest on him in the form of a dove. A voice came from heaven. It said, "You are my Son, and I love you. I am very pleased with you."   LUKE 3:21–22

Discussion Questions:

1. What is your favorite part of creation? What is the most beautiful thing you've ever seen in nature? Did that sight make you think of God? Why or why not?

2. Which person of the Trinity do you think is the easiest to understand: Father, Son or the Holy Spirit? Which do you think is the hardest to understand? Why?

3. Look at our key verse at the top of the chapter. What are the different ways each member of the Trinity relates to us? Which do you like best?

Personal God

⊶ KEY QUESTION:
Does God care about me?

⊶ KEY IDEA:
I believe God is involved in and cares about my daily life.

⊶ KEY VERSE:
I look up to the mountains.
　Where does my help come from?
My help comes from the Lord.
　He is the Maker of heaven and earth. *Psalm 121:1–2*

THINK ABOUT IT

The God of the Bible is the only true God—Father, Son and Holy Spirit. He created everything. He knows everything. But is he good? Does he care for us? Let's see what the Bible has to say.

God Is Good to Us

Have you ever prayed this prayer before your meal?

> *"God is great, God is good.*
> *Let us thank him for our food. Amen."*

Whether or not you pray for your meals that way, you might find it very easy to say "God is good." But do you really believe he is good? Is he good all the time? What about when you need something and you're not getting it? What about when you feel afraid? What about when you are getting bullied? Is God good even then?

There is an Old Testament Bible character who felt worried, fearful, even bullied! It was King David. When he was a young boy he was a shepherd, and he learned a lot about God by watching his sheep. He figured out that God is like a good shepherd who takes special care of his sheep, no matter what kind of situation they find themselves in. David wrote about this in the best-loved psalm in the Bible, Psalm 23.

> The LORD is my shepherd. He gives me everything I need.
>   He lets me lie down in fields of green grass.
> He leads me beside quiet waters.
>   He gives me new strength.
> He guides me in the right paths
>   for the honor of his name.
> Even though I walk
>   through the darkest valley,
> I will not be afraid.
>   You are with me.
> Your shepherd's rod and staff
>   comfort me.
>
> You prepare a feast for me
>   right in front of my enemies.
> You pour oil on my head.
>   My cup runs over.
> I am sure that your goodness and love will follow me
>   all the days of my life.
> And I will live in the house of the LORD
>   forever.   PSALM 23:1–6

God Cares for Us

When you think about how big God is, big enough to create the whole world, you might find it hard to imagine that he is paying any attention to you. Does he have time to care about that test you're about to take? Is he too busy to bother with your worry about your first practice with the new team? Do the things that matter to you matter to God?

It might surprise you to know that our great big God cares about everything you care about! Even the little things! God is not too big to care about every little thing. In fact, it is because he is so big that he is able to take care of everything at the same time! To help us imagine this, Jesus taught us to look around at how God takes care of birds and flowers. If he takes such good care of them, think of how much more he must care for us!

"I tell you, do not worry. Don't worry about your life and what you will eat or drink. And don't worry about your body and what you will wear. Isn't there more to life than eating? Aren't there more important things for the body than clothes? Look at the birds of the air. They don't plant or gather crops. They don't put away crops in storerooms. But your Father who is in heaven feeds them. Aren't you worth much more than they are? Can you add even one hour to your life by worrying?

"And why do you worry about clothes? See how the wild flowers grow. They don't work or make clothing. But here is what I tell you. Not even Solomon in all his royal robes was dressed like one of these flowers. If that is how God dresses the wild grass, won't he dress you even better? Your faith is so small! After all, the grass is here only today. Tomorrow it is thrown into the fire. So don't worry. Don't say, 'What will we eat?' Or, 'What will we drink?' Or, 'What will we wear?' People who are ungodly run after all those things. Your Father who is in heaven knows that you need them. But put God's kingdom first. Do what he wants you to do. Then all those things will also be given to you."   MATTHEW 6:25–33

> It might feel sometimes like God is far away. But Jesus did a special thing for us after he left the earth and returned to heaven. He sent the Holy Spirit to live inside us when we put our faith in him. Now we are never alone! It is the Holy Spirit who helps us live our lives according to God's plan for us. This doesn't mean life will always be easy. In fact, when it's not, it is reassuring to know that the Holy Spirit is there to help us and even to pray for us. No matter what happens, we have a promise from God that he will work it out for our good. We have a good and caring God.

The Holy Spirit helps us when we are weak. We don't know what we should pray for. But the Spirit himself prays for us. He prays through groans too deep for words. God, who looks into our hearts, knows the mind of the Spirit. And the Spirit prays for God's people just as God wants him to pray.

We know that in all things God works for the good of those who love him. He appointed them to be saved in keeping with his purpose.   ROMANS 8:26–28

I am absolutely sure that not even death or life can separate us from God's love. Not even angels or demons, the present or the future, or any powers can separate us. Not even the highest places or the lowest, or anything else in all creation can separate us. Nothing at all can ever separate us from God's love. That's because of what Christ Jesus our Lord has done.   ROMANS 8:38–39

Discussion Questions:

1. Why do you think the Bible calls Jesus a shepherd and his people sheep?

2. Our key verse calls God "the Maker of heaven and earth" — that's big! Does that make it harder or easier for you to trust that he will help you when you need it?

3. What do you worry about? What can you learn from flowers and birds to help you with your worry?

Salvation

⊶ KEY QUESTION:
How do I have a relationship with God?

⊶ KEY IDEA:
I believe a person can have a relationship with God by God's grace through faith in Jesus Christ.

⊶ KEY VERSE:
God's grace has saved you because of your faith in Christ. Your salvation doesn't come from anything you do. It is God's gift. It is not based on anything you have done. No one can brag about earning it. *Ephesians 2:8–9*

THINK ABOUT IT

We have discovered so far that God is the one true God: Father, Son and Holy Spirit. We have also discovered he is not far away and uninterested in our lives; he is personal and near. He is always good. He cares deeply for us. Now we ask what may be the most important question of all: "How do I have a relationship with God?"

Our Problem

At the beginning of the Bible in the Old Testament, God created the first man, Adam, and then the first woman, Eve. He gave them a beautiful place to live. It was called the Garden of Eden. This place was all theirs, except for one tree. One tree was off-limits. Satan disguised himself as a snake in the garden. He wanted to trick Adam and Eve into doing what God said not to do. His plan worked. Adam and Eve disobeyed God and ate fruit from the off-limits tree. This was the first sin, and we all are still dealing with the consequences of this sin. The consequence of sin is death and separation from God.

The LORD God had planted a garden in the east in Eden. He put in the garden the man he had formed. The LORD God made every kind of tree grow out of the ground. The trees were pleasing to look at. Their fruit was good to eat. There were two trees in the middle of the garden. One of them had fruit that let people live forever. The other had fruit that let people tell the difference between good and evil.   GENESIS 2:8–9

The LORD God put the man in the Garden of Eden. He put him there to farm its land and take care of it. The LORD God gave the man a command. He said, "You may eat fruit from any tree in the garden. But you must not eat the fruit from the tree of the knowledge of good and evil. If you do, you will certainly die."   GENESIS 2:15–17

The serpent was more clever than any of the wild animals the LORD God had made. The serpent said to the woman, "Did God really say, 'You must not eat fruit from any tree in the garden'?"

The woman said to the serpent, "We may eat fruit from the trees in the garden. But God did say, 'You must not eat the fruit from the tree in the middle of the garden. Do not even touch it. If you do, you will die.'"

"You will certainly not die," the serpent said to the woman. "God knows that when you eat fruit from that tree, you will know things you have never known before. Like God, you will be able to tell the difference between good and evil."

The woman saw that the tree's fruit was good to eat and pleasing to look at. She also saw that it would make a person wise. So she took some of the fruit and ate it. She also gave some to her husband, who was with her. And he ate it.   GENESIS 3:1–6

Then the LORD God said to the woman, "What have you done?"

The woman said, "The serpent tricked me. That's why I ate the fruit."   GENESIS 3:13

God's Solution

Human beings were certainly in a mess. That first sin got passed down to every human after that, and the consequence of sin is not being able to enjoy a relationship with our perfect God, here on earth or for eternity in heaven. But God did not abandon us. Before Adam and Eve even made their decision to sin, God already had a plan to save us from the consequences of that sin. In the New Testament, we learn that Jesus came to earth and, by living a perfect life and dying as we deserved to die, beat Satan. Jesus' death on a cross gave all of us a way to be forgiven for our sins once and for all. He gave all of us a way back to God.

From noon until three o'clock, the whole land was covered with darkness. About three o'clock, Jesus cried out in a loud voice. He said, *"Eli, Eli, lema sabachthani?"* This means "My God, my God, why have you deserted me?"

Some of those standing there heard Jesus cry out. They said, "He's calling for Elijah."

Right away one of them ran and got a sponge. He filled it with wine vinegar and put it on a stick. He offered it to Jesus to drink. The rest said, "Leave him alone. Let's see if Elijah comes to save him."

After Jesus cried out again in a loud voice, he died.

At that moment the temple curtain was torn in two from top to bottom. The earth shook. The rocks split. Tombs broke open. The bodies of many holy people who had died were raised to life. They came out of the tombs. After Jesus was raised from the dead, they went into the holy city. There they appeared to many people.

The Roman commander and those guarding Jesus saw the earthquake and all that had happened. They were terrified. They exclaimed, "He was surely the Son of God!"   Matthew 27:45–54

The Sabbath day was now over. It was dawn on the first day of the week. Mary Magdalene and the other Mary went to look at the tomb.

There was a powerful earthquake. An angel of the Lord came down from heaven. The angel went to the tomb. He rolled back the stone and sat on it. His body shone like lightning. His clothes were as white as snow. The guards were so afraid of him that they shook and became like dead men.

The angel said to the women, "Don't be afraid. I know that you are looking for Jesus, who was crucified. He is not here! He has risen, just as he said he would! Come and see the place where he was lying. Go quickly! Tell his disciples, 'He has risen from the dead. He is going ahead of you into Galilee. There you will see him.' Now I have told you."   Matthew 28:1–7

The Promise

In perhaps the most famous single verse in the whole Bible, Jesus explains our problem (we are going to die), God's solution (God loved us so much he gave his Son to die in our place), and the promise (if we believe in him we will live forever with him).

God so loved the world that he gave his one and only Son. Anyone who believes in him will not die but will have eternal life.

JOHN 3:16

Discussion Questions:

1. Why do you think Adam and Eve chose to eat the forbidden fruit? What do you think you would have done if you had been in their position?

2. Our key verse says our salvation doesn't come from anything we do. What are some things people do to try to make sure they are saved? What really saves people according to John 3:16?

3. Have you asked Jesus to be your personal Savior? If so, share about your experience. If not, what are you waiting for?

The Bible

KEY QUESTION:
How do I know God and his plan for my life?

KEY IDEA:
I believe the Bible is God's Word and it guides my beliefs and actions.

KEY VERSE:
God has breathed life into all Scripture. It is useful for teaching us what is true. It is useful for correcting our mistakes. It is useful for making our lives whole again. It is useful for training us to do what is right. By using Scripture, the servant of God can be completely prepared to do every good thing. *2 Timothy 3:16–17*

THINK ABOUT IT

How do we figure out where we came from and why we are here? How do we know right from wrong? How do we have enough power to face challenges? The answer is spelled B-I-B-L-E. Our job is to read it and believe.

"The Bible is useful for making our lives whole again."

Our key verse lists several ways the Bible is useful. In the Old Testament, Moses experienced God's Word making his life whole again. When we first see Moses in this story, he was taking care of a flock in the desert, forty years after running away from a murder charge. That's a long way from his life of prestige and importance as Pharaoh's adopted son in Egypt! But God, in a dramatic way, gives Moses a special assignment—a new

*plan for his life. When Moses obeys, God makes him the great
leader he was destined to be.*

Moses was taking care of the flock of his father-in-law Jethro.
Jethro was the priest of Midian. Moses led the flock to the western side of the desert. He came to Horeb. It was the mountain of
God. There the angel of the LORD appeared to him from inside a
burning bush. Moses saw that the bush was on fire. But it didn't
burn up. So Moses thought, "I'll go over and see this strange sight.
Why doesn't the bush burn up?"

The LORD saw that Moses had gone over to look. So God spoke
to him from inside the bush. He called out, "Moses! Moses!"

"Here I am," Moses said.

"Do not come any closer," God said. "Take off your sandals.
The place you are standing on is holy ground." He continued, "I
am the God of your father. I am the God of Abraham. I am the
God of Isaac. And I am the God of Jacob." When Moses heard
that, he turned his face away. He was afraid to look at God.

The LORD said, "I have seen how my people are suffering in
Egypt. I have heard them cry out because of their slave drivers. I
am concerned about their suffering. So I have come down to save
them from the Egyptians. I will bring them up out of that land. I
will bring them into a good land. It has a lot of room. It is a land
that has plenty of milk and honey."   EXODUS 3:1–8A

"So now, go. I am sending you to Pharaoh. I want you to bring
the Israelites out of Egypt. They are my people."   EXODUS 3:10

"The Bible is useful for training us to do what is right."

*According to our key verse, the Bible is also useful for training
us to do what is right. We see that most clearly several months
after Moses met God in a burning bush. This time, Moses found
himself on a mountaintop, meeting God again. God gave him
a set of stone tablets upon which God had written with his own
finger. What was so important that God wanted to write it in
stone? We call it the Ten Commandments. These ten simple
instructions formed the guidelines for living that generations*

of people have followed. They have given us the standard by
which we know right from wrong.

Here are all the words God spoke. He said,

"I am the LORD your God. I brought you out of Egypt. That is the land where you were slaves.

"Do not put any other gods in place of me.

"Do not make for yourself statues of gods that look like anything in the sky. They may not look like anything on the earth or in the waters either. Do not bow down to them or worship them. I, the LORD your God, am a jealous God. I cause the sins of the parents to affect their children. I will cause the sins of those who hate me to affect even their grandchildren and great-grandchildren. But for all time to come I show love to all those who love me and keep my commandments.

"Do not misuse the name of the LORD your God. The LORD will find guilty anyone who misuses his name.

"Remember to keep the Sabbath day holy. Do all your work in six days. But the seventh day is a sabbath to honor the LORD your God. Do not do any work on that day. The same command applies to your sons and daughters, your male and female servants,

and your animals. It also applies to any outsiders who live in your towns. In six days the LORD made the heavens, the earth, the sea and everything in them. But he rested on the seventh day. So the LORD blessed the Sabbath day and made it holy.

"Honor your father and mother. Then you will live a long time in the land the LORD your God is giving you.

"Do not murder.

"Do not commit adultery.

"Do not steal.

"Do not be a false witness against your neighbor.

"Do not want to have anything your neighbor owns. Do not want to have your neighbor's house, wife, male or female servant, ox or donkey."   EXODUS 20:1–17

"By using Scripture, the servant of God can be completely prepared to do every good thing."

Our key verse says the Bible is where we can find direction for our lives, as Moses did at the burning bush. It also says the Bible trains us to do the right thing, as the Ten Commandments do. And our key verse ends by saying that when we use the Bible (Scripture), we can be "completely prepared to do every good thing." There is no better example of that than when Jesus used God's Word as his only weapon to fight off the devil. He needed nothing else. When Satan attacked, he was "completely prepared" with a counter-attack from God's Word. Like a skilled swordsman, Jesus resisted and defeated his enemy. Let's watch the master at work!

The Holy Spirit led Jesus into the desert. There the devil tempted him. After 40 days and 40 nights of going without eating, Jesus was hungry. The tempter came to him. He said, "If you are the Son of God, tell these stones to become bread."

Jesus answered, "It is written, 'Man must not live only on bread. He must also live on every word that comes from the mouth of God.'"

Then the devil took Jesus to the holy city. He had him stand on the highest point of the temple. "If you are the Son of God," he said, "throw yourself down. It is written,

" 'The Lord will command his angels to take good care
        of you.
    They will lift you up in their hands.
    Then you won't trip over a stone.' "

Jesus answered him, "It is also written, 'Do not test the Lord
your God.' "
Finally, the devil took Jesus to a very high mountain. He
showed him all the kingdoms of the world and their glory. "If you
bow down and worship me," he said, "I will give you all this."
Jesus said to him, "Get away from me, Satan! It is written,
'Worship the Lord your God. He is the only one you should
serve.' "
Then the devil left Jesus. Angels came and took care of him.

MATTHEW 4:1–11

Discussion Questions:

1. Name the five ways our key verse says the Bible is useful.
   Which of the five do you need the most right now? Why?

2. Assuming the first commandment is the most important
   one, why do you think the first commandment is "Do not
   put any other gods in place of me"? What are some things
   you sometimes make more important than God in your
   life?

3. You may someday encounter someone who tries to twist
   Scripture, who tries to convince you that the Bible says
   something it doesn't say, just like the devil did with Jesus.
   What can you do to make sure you don't fall for it?

5

Identity in Christ

KEY QUESTION:
Who am I?

KEY IDEA:
I believe I am significant because I am a child of God.

KEY VERSE:
Some people did accept him and did believe in his name. He gave them the right to become children of God.

John 1:12

THINK ABOUT IT

Our key question asks, Who am I? The answer to that question is what we call our identity. Although "who am I?" could be answered by describing our looks, talents, family, or character qualities, our real identity in Christ goes beyond that. We will discover that—when we believe and receive God's gift of grace— we become a new person with a new identity. We are treasured because we are children of God.

Our New Name

The names in the Bible have meanings, and the meaning of a name tells us a lot about the person's character or background. For instance, did you know there was someone in the Bible whose name meant "he laughs"? Abraham and Sarah were told by God to name their son Isaac, "he laughs," and you'll see why in the following Old Testament story.

You're also going to see two examples of God giving someone a new name. He renamed Abram [exalted father] to

Abraham [father of many]. He renamed Abram's wife Sarai [my princess] to Sarah [princess of many families]. Whenever God gave a person a new name, it was his way of showing that the person had experienced a change of heart or was given a new life purpose. A new name was a signal of a new identity.

When Abram was 99 years old, the LORD appeared to him. He said, "I am the Mighty God. Walk faithfully with me. Live in a way that pleases me. I will now act on my covenant between me and you. I will greatly increase the number of your children after you."

Abram fell with his face to the ground. God said to him, "This is my covenant with you. You will be the father of many nations. You will not be called Abram anymore. Your name will be Abraham, because I have made you a father of many nations. I will greatly increase the number of your children after you. Nations and kings will come from you. I will make my covenant with you last forever. It will be between me and you and your family after you for all time to come. I will be your God. And I will be the God of all your family after you."   GENESIS 17:1–7

God also said to Abraham, "Do not continue to call your wife by the name Sarai. Her name will be Sarah. I will give her my blessing. You can be sure that I will give you a son by her. I will bless her so that she will be the mother of nations. Kings of nations will come from her."

Abraham fell with his face to the ground. He laughed and said to himself, "Can a 100-year-old man have a son? Can Sarah have a child at the age of 90?"   GENESIS 17:15–17

The LORD was gracious to Sarah, just as he had said he would be. The LORD did for Sarah what he had promised to do. Sarah became pregnant. She had a son by Abraham when he was old. The child was born at the exact time God had promised. Abraham gave the name Isaac to the son Sarah had by him. When his son Isaac was eight days old, Abraham circumcised him. He did it exactly as God had commanded him. Abraham was 100 years old when his son Isaac was born to him.

Sarah said, "God has given laughter to me. Everyone who hears about this will laugh with me."   Genesis 21:1–6

Our Adoption

These days our first names don't usually give clues as to our identity quite the way they did in Bible times. But, our last names certainly do! Our last name tells people what family we belong to. And if you were adopted, your last name was changed from your birth name to your adoptive family's name. Your identity changed when you were adopted.

Did you know the Bible says God the Father chose to adopt us? You might have heard Christians referred to as "children of God." The way we became his children was by being spiritually adopted! The passage you're about to read contains our key verse, and it says we are called "children of God" because of

what God does. And what does God do, exactly? He chooses us to be adopted, as you'll see in the following verses. The last verse might remind you of adoptions that take place from orphanages in a faraway country. How wonderful to be members of God's family!

Some people did accept him and did believe in his name. He gave them the right to become children of God. To be a child of God has nothing to do with human parents. Children of God are not born because of human choice or because a husband wants them to be born. They are born because of what God does.

JOHN 1:12–13

God chose us to belong to Christ before the world was created. He chose us to be holy and without blame in his eyes. He loved us. So he decided long ago to adopt us. He adopted us as his children with all the rights children have. He did it because of what Jesus Christ has done. It pleased God to do it.   EPHESIANS 1:4–5

So you are no longer outsiders and strangers. You are citizens together with God's people. You are also members of God's family.   EPHESIANS 2:19

Our New Identity

The verse we just read says that when we become members of God's family, we are "no longer outsiders and strangers." Have you ever felt like an outsider and a stranger? Zacchaeus the tax collector certainly did. In Jesus' time, tax collectors were hated because they worked for Rome and took money from the Jews. Shockingly, Jesus didn't treat Zacchaeus like an outsider and a stranger like everyone else did. Instead, he went home with him! Zacchaeus had a change of heart, and that dramatically changed how he behaved. That's what happens when you are adopted into the family of God; you become a different person.

Jesus entered Jericho and was passing through. A man named Zacchaeus lived there. He was a chief tax collector and was very rich. Zacchaeus wanted to see who Jesus was. But he was a short

man. He could not see Jesus because of the crowd. So he ran ahead and climbed a sycamore-fig tree. He wanted to see Jesus, who was coming that way.

Jesus reached the spot where Zacchaeus was. He looked up and said, "Zacchaeus, come down at once. I must stay at your house today." So Zacchaeus came down at once and welcomed him gladly.

All the people saw this. They began to whisper among themselves. They said, "Jesus has gone to be the guest of a sinner."

But Zacchaeus stood up. He said, "Look, Lord! Here and now I give half of what I own to those who are poor. And if I have cheated anybody out of anything, I will pay it back. I will pay back four times the amount I took."

Jesus said to Zacchaeus, "Today salvation has come to your house. You are a member of Abraham's family line."   LUKE 19:1–9

Discussion Questions:

1. What is one of your best character qualities? Are you kind? Brave? Patient? Thankful? Give yourself a new name based on your best trait. How would you feel being called that name from now on?

2. Go back and read Ephesians 1:4–5. Why did God adopt us? How does God feel about us? What does our key verse, John 1:12, say is our part in becoming children of God?

3. When we are given a new identity we may start behaving differently. If you have become a child of God, what is different about you?

Church

🔑 KEY QUESTION:
How will God accomplish his plan?

🔑 KEY IDEA:
I believe God uses the church to bring about his plan.

🔑 KEY VERSE:
We will speak the truth in love. So we will grow up in every way to become the body of Christ. Christ is the head of the body. *Ephesians 4:15*

THINK ABOUT IT

God created a community called the church for those of us who are Christians. We might think of the church as a building, but in the Bible, the word "church" was not used to describe a building. The church is people, people who are in the family of God, and it is the church of his people that God uses to accomplish his plans.

Our Family Tree

We learned in the last chapter about our new identity as children of God. Do you know another name for all of God's children? We are called the church! If you trace the church back to where we began, just as if you were tracing your family tree, you would have to go back before Jesus. In fact, you would go all the way back to Abraham. Do you remember from the last chapter why Abram was given the new name of Abraham? It was to signify the promise God made to him, the promise to

45

*change him from an "exalted father" to a "father of many." And
it would be from Abraham's descendants that the church would
eventually be started.*

The LORD had said to Abram, "Go from your country, your
people and your father's family. Go to the land I will show you.

> "I will make you into a great nation,
>   and I will bless you.
> I will make your name great.
>   You will be a blessing to others.
> I will bless those who bless you.
>   I will put a curse on anyone who puts a curse on you.
> All nations on earth
>   will be blessed because of you."   GENESIS 12:1–3

The LORD took Abram outside and said, "Look up at the sky.
Count the stars, if you can." Then he said to him, "That's how
many children will be born into your family."

Abram believed the LORD. The LORD was pleased with Abram because he believed. So Abram's faith made him right with the LORD. GENESIS 15:5–6

Church? What's a Church?

God promised Abraham many children. When God said "children," he meant many generations. Jesus was a descendant of Abraham. He is one of these children. When we choose to follow Jesus, we become adopted into this family. We become Abraham's children too.

We are going to read about the moment in the New Testament when the disciples first learned from Jesus about this new idea of "church." They didn't understand it yet, but they would become the church. The church is not a building. The church is all those who have been adopted into Abraham's family through Jesus.

Jesus went to the area of Caesarea Philippi. There he asked his disciples, "Who do people say the Son of Man is?"

They replied, "Some say John the Baptist. Others say Elijah. Still others say Jeremiah, or one of the prophets."

"But what about you?" he asked. "Who do you say I am?"

Simon Peter answered, "You are the Messiah. You are the Son of the living God."

Jesus replied, "Blessed are you, Simon, son of Jonah! No mere human showed this to you. My Father in heaven showed it to you. Here is what I tell you. You are Peter. On this rock I will build my church." MATTHEW 16:13–18A

Imagine how strange that must have sounded to the disciples! "I will build my church? What's a church?" It was as if Jesus was dropping hints about a mystery they couldn't figure out yet. But it would soon make sense. After Jesus came back to life after his death on the cross, he told his disciples that they would receive the gift of the Holy Spirit. Another hint! They would soon realize that only when the Holy Spirit arrived would they be given the power it would take to start the church.

One day Jesus was eating with them. He gave them a command. "Do not leave Jerusalem," he said. "Wait for the gift my Father promised. You have heard me talk about it. John baptized with water. But in a few days you will be baptized with the Holy Spirit."   Acts 1:4–5

"You will receive power when the Holy Spirit comes on you. Then you will tell people about me in Jerusalem, and in all Judea and Samaria. And you will even tell other people about me from one end of the earth to the other."

After Jesus said this, he was taken up to heaven. The apostles watched until a cloud hid him from their sight.   Acts 1:8–9

The Church Is Born

After Jesus rose up into heaven, his followers continued to meet together and pray together. They knew they were waiting for the Holy Spirit, but what would happen when he came was still a mystery to them. Imagine their surprise when the events of the day of Pentecost unfolded! Now they knew why the Holy Spirit had to come. The power he gave them was irresistible, and thousands of people formed the first church that very day.

When the day of Pentecost came, all the believers gathered in one place. Suddenly a sound came from heaven. It was like a strong wind blowing. It filled the whole house where they were sitting. They saw something that looked like fire in the shape of tongues. The flames separated and came to rest on each of them. All of them were filled with the Holy Spirit. They began to speak in languages they had not known before. The Spirit gave them the ability to do this.

Godly Jews from every country in the world were staying in Jerusalem. A crowd came together when they heard the sound. They were bewildered because each of them heard their own language being spoken. The crowd was really amazed. They asked, "Aren't all these people who are speaking Galileans? Then why do we each hear them speaking in our own native language?"

Acts 2:1–8

Peter stood up, raised his voice, and spoke to the crowd. He told them how Jesus fulfilled the ancient prophecies about the Messiah, yet, he was put to death. But it was impossible for death to keep its hold on him, and God raised him, and later sent the Holy Spirit—on that very day! At the end of his message, there was an astonishing response.

"So be sure of this, all you people of Israel. You nailed Jesus to the cross. But God has made him both Lord and Messiah."

When the people heard this, it had a deep effect on them. They said to Peter and the other apostles, "Brothers, what should we do?"

Peter replied, "All of you must turn away from your sins and be baptized in the name of Jesus Christ. Then your sins will be forgiven. You will receive the gift of the Holy Spirit. The promise is for you and your children. It is also for all who are far away. It is for all whom the Lord our God will choose."

Peter said many other things to warn them. He begged them, "Save yourselves from these evil people." Those who accepted his message were baptized. About 3,000 people joined the believers that day.   ACTS 2:36–41

Discussion Questions:

1. What term does our key verse, Ephesians 4:15, use for the church? Why is that a good way to describe what the church is?

2. Our key verse says that the way we grow up and become the body of Christ is by speaking the truth to each other in love. That's just what Peter did on the day of Pentecost. What are some other ways we can speak the truth in love?

3. Have you ever felt the Holy Spirit working in your life? Share about it.

Humanity

How does God see us?

I believe all people are loved by God and need Jesus Christ as their Savior.

God so loved the world that he gave his one and only Son. Anyone who believes in him will not die but will have eternal life.

John 3:16

THINK ABOUT IT

God created everything, but the high point of creation was when he made human beings. Humanity is special, and the Bible is the record of the love story between God and humans. In this love story though, there was a sinister plot by a wicked enemy who came between God and us. But God pursued us anyway, with enough love for everyone.

Things Went from Bad to Worse

God made human beings, and at first he enjoyed a perfect and harmonious relationship with them. Then Satan deceived Eve, and she and Adam chose to go against God, and things were never the same. This was the world's first sin. This sin led to many consequences, one of which was this: Every human in every generation after Adam and Eve would be born into a broken world. Never again would humanity experience the pure and perfect connection with God that existed before there was sin.

Right away things went from bad to worse. Adam and Eve's sons, Cain and Abel, showed us that sin not only broke our relationship with God, it also had a terrible effect on the way we treat each other—even those we love.

Abel took care of sheep. Cain farmed the land. After some time, Cain gathered some things he had grown. He brought them as an offering to the LORD. And Abel also brought an offering. He brought the fattest parts of some animals from his flock. They were the first animals born to their mothers. The LORD was pleased with Abel and his offering. But he wasn't pleased with Cain and his offering. So Cain became very angry, and his face was sad.

Then the LORD said to Cain, "Why are you angry? Why are you looking so sad? Do what is right and then you will be accepted. If you don't do what is right, sin is waiting at your door to grab you. It desires to control you. But you must rule over it."

Cain said to his brother Abel, "Let's go out to the field." So they went out. There Cain attacked his brother Abel and killed him.

Then the LORD said to Cain, "Where is your brother Abel?"

"I don't know," Cain replied. "Am I supposed to take care of my brother?"

The LORD said, "What have you done? Listen! Your brother's blood is crying out to me from the ground. So I am putting a curse on you. I am driving you away from this ground. It has opened its mouth to receive your brother's blood from your hand. When you farm the land, it will not produce its crops for you anymore. You will be a restless person who wanders around on the earth."

Cain said to the LORD, "You are punishing me more than I can take. Today you are driving me away from the land. I will be hidden from you. I'll be a restless person who wanders around on the earth. Anyone who finds me will kill me."

But the LORD said to him, "No. Anyone who kills you will be paid back seven times." The LORD put a mark on Cain. Then anyone who found him wouldn't kill him. So Cain went away from the LORD. He lived in the land of Nod. It was east of Eden. GENESIS 4:2B–16

Anyone and Everyone

How terrible! The first murder was committed by the first brother! But did you notice something surprising? God didn't give up on Cain. He protected him, even though his sin drove him away from God.

Ever since that time, humans have started out separated from God. But God doesn't give up on us, just like he didn't give up on Cain. Even when we mess up, we can still return to God. This is all thanks to Jesus. Because Jesus died on the cross, God's family is open to everyone. In the New Testament, John makes this clear in his Gospel. Notice how these verses use words like "anyone" and "everyone" to tell us who can be in God's family. Starting with our key verse, we see that Jesus offers salvation to every single person on earth.

God so loved the world that he gave his one and only Son. Anyone who believes in him will not die but will have eternal life.

JOHN 3:16

"**Anyone** who believes in the Son has eternal life. **Anyone** who does not believe in the Son will not have life. God's anger remains on them."   John 3:36

"But **anyone** who drinks the water I give them will never be thirsty. In fact, the water I give them will become a spring of water in them. It will flow up into eternal life."   John 4:14

"What I'm about to tell you is true. **Anyone** who hears my word and believes him who sent me has eternal life. They will not be judged. They have crossed over from death to life."   John 5:24

"**Everyone** the Father gives me will come to me. I will never send away **anyone** who comes to me."   John 6:37

"I am the living bread that came down from heaven. **Everyone** who eats some of this bread will live forever. This bread is my body. I will give it for the life of **the world**."   John 6:51

Jesus spoke to the people again. He said, "I am the light of **the world**. **Anyone** who follows me will never walk in darkness. They will have that light. They will have life."   John 8:12

"What I'm about to tell you is true. **Whoever** obeys my word will never die."   John 8:51

Aren't those verses incredible? God's love is so huge. He loves us, no matter what we have done. He does not want to lose any of us, not even one! Remember how we likened the story of humanity to a love story, where a wicked enemy comes between us and God, and God loves us so much he pursues us so he can have a relationship with us again? That's just what happens in Jesus' story of the wandering sheep that got separated from the shepherd. Imagine how much God loves every single one of us!

"What do you think? Suppose a man owns 100 sheep and one of them wanders away. Won't he leave the 99 sheep on the hills?

Won't he go and look for the one that wandered off? What I'm about to tell you is true. If he finds that sheep, he is happier about the one than about the 99 that didn't wander off. It is the same with your Father in heaven. He does not want any of these little ones to die."   MATTHEW 18:12–14

Discussion Questions:

1. Go back to the Anyone and Everyone section and read it out loud, substituting your name for words such as "the world" or "anyone" or "everyone." How does it feel to know that YOU are included in "anyone" and "everyone?" Have you said yes to God's offer of love to you?

2. Based on what you have read in this chapter, what is the answer to our key question, "How does God see us?"

3. If God loves anyone and everyone, then we should too. But is there someone you have a hard time loving? If so, what small act of kindness can you do for them this week to help change your attitude and start loving them the way God loves them?

Compassion

KEY QUESTION:
What should we do about people in need?

KEY IDEA:
I believe God calls all Christians to show compassion to people in need.

KEY VERSE:
Stand up for the weak and for children whose fathers
    have died.
   Protect the rights of people who are poor or treated
     badly.
Save those who are weak and needy.
   Save them from the power of sinful people. *Psalm 82:3–4*

THINK ABOUT IT

Our belief in humanity calls us to love anyone and everyone the way God does. Compassion goes a step further by asking us to feel their pain. Compassion is a word that means "suffer with." God wants us to get close to people who are suffering and suffer with them so they are not alone. We might not be able to fix the problem, but we can try to understand their pain.

Protect the Poor

Our key verse, Psalm 82:3–4, says, "Protect the rights of the people who are poor or treated badly." There is a man in the Old Testament named Boaz who did just that. Boaz was a landowner who made sure his harvesters left grain behind as a way of showing compassion to people in need. When a young

widow named Ruth showed up to pick up leftover grain to feed
herself and her widowed mother-in-law Naomi, Boaz went the
extra mile and offered her protection. As you read this story of
Boaz's compassion, look for the ways Ruth also showed com-
passion.

Naomi had a relative on her husband's side of the family. The
relative's name was Boaz. He was a very important man from the
family of Elimelek.

Ruth, who was from Moab, spoke to Naomi. Ruth said, "Let
me go out to the fields. I'll pick up the grain that has been left. I'll
do it behind anyone who is pleased with me."

Naomi said to her, "My daughter, go ahead." So Ruth went out
to a field and began to pick up grain. She worked behind those
cutting and gathering the grain. As it turned out, she was working in a field that belonged to Boaz. He was from the family of
Elimelek.

Just then Boaz arrived from Bethlehem. He greeted those cutting and gathering the grain. He said, "May the LORD be with you!"

"And may the LORD bless you!" they replied.

Boaz spoke to the man in charge of his workers. He asked, "Who does that young woman belong to?"

The man replied, "She's from Moab. She came back from there with Naomi. The young woman said, 'Please let me walk behind the workers. Let me pick up the grain that is left.' She came into the field. She has kept on working here from morning until now. She took only one short rest in the shade."

So Boaz said to Ruth, "Dear woman, listen to me. Don't pick up grain in any other field. Don't go anywhere else. Stay here with the women who work for me. Keep your eye on the field where the men are cutting grain. Walk behind the women who are gathering it. Pick up the grain that is left. I've told the men not to bother you. When you are thirsty, go and get a drink. Take water from the jars the men have filled."

When Ruth heard that, she bowed down with her face to the ground. She asked him, "Why are you being so kind to me? In fact, why are you even noticing me? I'm from another country."

Boaz replied, "I've been told all about you. I've heard about everything you have done for your mother-in-law since your husband died. I know that you left your father and mother. I know that you left your country. You came to live with people you didn't know before. May the LORD reward you for what you have done. May the LORD, the God of Israel, bless you richly. You have come to him to find safety under his care."

"Sir, I hope you will continue to be kind to me," Ruth said. "You have made me feel safe. You have spoken kindly to me. And I'm not even as important as one of your servants!"   RUTH 2:1–13

Ruth got up to pick up more grain. Then Boaz gave orders to his men. He said, "Let her take some stalks from what the women have tied up. Don't tell her she can't. Even pull out some stalks for her. Leave them for her to pick up. Don't tell her she shouldn't do it."

So Ruth picked up grain in the field until evening. Then she separated the barley from the straw. The barley weighed 30 pounds. She carried it back to town. Her mother-in-law saw how much she had gathered. Ruth also brought out the food left over from the lunch Boaz had given her. She gave it to Naomi.

Her mother-in-law asked her, "Where did you pick up grain today? Where did you work? May the man who noticed you be blessed!"

Then Ruth told her about the man whose field she had worked in. "The name of the man I worked with today is Boaz," she said.

"May the LORD bless him!" Naomi said to her daughter-in-law. "The LORD is still being kind to those who are living and those who are dead." She continued, "That man is a close relative of ours. He's one of our family protectors."   RUTH 2:15–20

Save the Weak and Needy

Another way to show compassion is mentioned in our key verse: "Save those who are weak and needy." Probably the best-known story of someone who saved the weak and needy is the story in the New Testament of the Good Samaritan. Jesus told this story to help people see that the person who loves God the best is not the one who is the most strict about obeying the law but the one who shows compassion.

One day an authority on the law stood up to test Jesus. "Teacher," he asked, "what must I do to receive eternal life?"

"What is written in the Law?" Jesus replied. "How do you understand it?"

He answered, "'Love the Lord your God with all your heart and with all your soul. Love him with all your strength and with all your mind.' And, 'Love your neighbor as you love yourself.'"

"You have answered correctly," Jesus replied. "Do that, and you will live."

But the man wanted to make himself look good. So he asked Jesus, "And who is my neighbor?"

Jesus replied, "A man was going down from Jerusalem to Jericho. Robbers attacked him. They stripped off his clothes and beat him. Then they went away, leaving him almost dead. A priest happened to be going down that same road. When he saw the man, he passed by on the other side. A Levite also came by. When he saw the man, he passed by on the other side too. But a Samaritan came to the place where the man was. When he saw the man, he felt sorry for him. He went to him, poured olive oil and wine

on his wounds and bandaged them. Then he put the man on his own donkey. He brought him to an inn and took care of him. The next day he took out two silver coins. He gave them to the owner of the inn. 'Take care of him,' he said. 'When I return, I will pay you back for any extra expense you may have.'

"Which of the three do you think was a neighbor to the man who was attacked by robbers?"

The authority on the law replied, "The one who felt sorry for him."

Jesus told him, "Go and do as he did."   LUKE 10:25–37

Discussion Questions:

1. Share about a time when someone showed you compassion. How did this make you feel?

2. Share about a time when you showed compassion to someone else. How did this make you feel?

3. Review the kinds of people our key verse, Psalm 82:3–4, talks about. Do you know anyone who can be described in one of those ways? If so, what can you do to show them compassion this week?

Stewardship

⊙—🔑 KEY QUESTION:
What is God's call on my life?

⊙—🔑 KEY IDEA:
I believe everything I am and everything I own belong to God.

⊙—🔑 KEY VERSE:

The earth belongs to the LORD. And so does everything
in it.
The world belongs to him. And so do all those who
live in it.
He set it firmly on the oceans.
He made it secure on the waters.   *Psalm 24:1–2*

THINK ABOUT IT

Our key question is answered by the chapter title. What is God's call on my life? Stewardship. A steward is someone who takes care of property for the owner. The property doesn't belong to the steward; it belongs to the owner. Everything in the earth belongs to the Lord, and God has called us to be good caretakers for him. Knowing we are stewards and not owners makes it easier to give things away to help others because they don't belong to us anyway!

God Called Us To Be Stewards

God gave Adam and Eve one assignment: to rule over everything he had placed on the earth. God told them to bring the earth under their control and to rule over every living creature. Those words "control" and "rule over" describe what a steward does. So God's call on their life (and on ours) was to be good stewards of all the gifts on the earth he offered to them to enjoy.

God blessed them. He said to them, "Have children so that there will be many of you. Fill the earth and bring it under your control. Rule over the fish in the seas and the birds in the sky. Rule over every living creature that moves along the ground."

Then God said, "I am giving you every plant on the face of the whole earth that produces its own seeds. I am giving you every tree that has fruit with seeds in it. All of them will be given to you for food. I am giving every green plant as food for all the land animals and for all the birds in the sky. I am also giving the plants to all the creatures that move along the ground. I am giving them to every living thing that breathes." And that's exactly what happened.   GENESIS 1:28–30

Giving God What Is His Already

We are going to read two stories of women who were extreme givers. The first story from the Old Testament might seem shocking at first. Hannah wanted a child so badly she promised that if God gave her a child then she would give the child back to God. God answered her prayer, and she kept her promise and gave her young son to God. That might seem extreme, but Hannah knew that everything belonged to God—even her child. She was so thankful that God allowed her the joy of having a baby she wanted to express her thankfulness by giving him back to God. She understood that she was a steward, not an owner, of the many blessings God had given her, and she was simply giving God what was his already.

One time when they had finished eating and drinking in Shiloh, Hannah stood up. Eli the priest was sitting on his chair by the doorpost of the LORD's house. Hannah was very sad. She wept and wept. She prayed to the LORD. She made a promise to him. She said, "LORD, you rule over all. Please see how I'm suffering! Show concern for me! Don't forget about me! Please give me a son! If you do, I'll give him back to the LORD. Then he will serve the LORD all the days of his life. He'll never use a razor on his head. He'll never cut his hair."

As Hannah kept on praying to the LORD, Eli watched her lips. She was praying in her heart. Her lips were moving. But she wasn't making a sound. Eli thought Hannah was drunk. He said to her, "How long are you going to stay drunk? Stop drinking your wine."

"That's not true, sir," Hannah replied. "I'm a woman who is deeply troubled. I haven't been drinking wine or beer. I was telling the LORD all my troubles. Don't think of me as an evil woman. I've been praying here because I'm very sad. My pain is so great."

Eli answered, "Go in peace. May the God of Israel give you what you have asked him for."

She said, "May you be pleased with me." Then she left and had something to eat. Her face wasn't sad anymore.

Early the next morning Elkanah and his family got up. They worshiped the LORD. Then they went back to their home

in Ramah. Elkanah slept with his wife Hannah. And the LORD
blessed her. So after some time, Hannah became pregnant. She
had a baby boy. She said, "I asked the LORD for him." So she
named him Samuel.   1 SAMUEL 1:9–20

When the boy didn't need her to breast-feed him anymore,
she took him with her to Shiloh. She took him there even though
he was still very young. She brought him to the LORD's house.
She brought along a bull that was three years old. She brought 36
pounds of flour. She also brought a bottle of wine. The bottle was
made out of animal skin. After the bull was sacrificed, Elkanah
and Hannah brought the boy to Eli. Hannah said to Eli, "Pardon
me, sir. I'm the woman who stood here beside you praying to the
LORD. And that's just as sure as you are alive. I prayed for this
child. The LORD has given me what I asked him for. So now I'm
giving him to the LORD. As long as he lives he'll be given to the
LORD." And there Eli worshiped the LORD.   1 SAMUEL 1:24–28

*The story doesn't end there. Because Hannah was such a good
steward, God continued to bless her.*

The boy Samuel served the LORD. He wore a sacred linen
apron. Each year his mother made him a little robe. She took it
to him when she went up to Shiloh with her husband. She did
it when her husband went to offer the yearly sacrifice. Eli would
bless Elkanah and his wife. He would say, "May the LORD give you
children by this woman. May they take the place of the boy she
prayed for and gave to the LORD." Then they would go home. The
LORD was gracious to Hannah. Over a period of years she had
three more sons and two daughters. During that whole time the
boy Samuel grew up serving the LORD.   1 SAMUEL 2:18–21

*The second woman who was an extreme giver was the poor
widow Jesus noticed at the temple. Even though the amount of
her gift was quite small, it was all she had. That's extreme! The
Bible is clear that stewardship is not about how much we give.
Instead, stewardship is about what is going on in our hearts. By
giving God what was his already, this woman was showing faith
that God would take care of her.*

Jesus sat down across from the place where people put their temple offerings. He watched the crowd putting their money into the offering boxes. Many rich people threw large amounts into them. But a poor widow came and put in two very small copper coins. They were worth only a few pennies.

Jesus asked his disciples to come to him. He said, "What I'm about to tell you is true. That poor widow has put more into the offering box than all the others. They all gave a lot because they are rich. But she gave even though she is poor. She put in everything she had. That was all she had to live on."   MARK 12:41–44

Discussion Questions:

1. Think of one of your favorite possessions. Do you treat it as if you were its owner or its steward? What do you need to change in order to act more like a steward?

2. When you act like an owner of your possessions, what problems does it cause between you and others?

3. Why would someone prefer to be a steward and not an owner? What are some of the good things about being a steward? What are some of the problems of being an owner?

Eternity

🔑 KEY QUESTION:

What happens next?

🔑 KEY IDEA:

I believe there is a heaven and a hell and that Jesus will return to establish his eternal kingdom.

🔑 KEY VERSE:

Do not let your hearts be troubled. You believe in God. Believe in me also. There are many rooms in my Father's house. If this were not true, would I have told you that I am going there? Would I have told you that I would prepare a place for you there?   *John 14:1–2*

THINK ABOUT IT

The first nine beliefs in this book are preparation for the tenth —the belief in eternity. Life on earth is a rehearsal for eternity in heaven. God has given us our beliefs to help us become more like him. The more we practice living out our beliefs, the closer to God we get. But while living on earth we will never get as close to him as Adam and Eve were before they sinned. God is preparing a wonderful place for us so that after we die we will be able to enjoy life with him as he has always wanted to give us.

A Chariot Came for Elijah

People in Old Testament times were not taught as much about heaven as those in the New Testament. We do, however, get one dramatic glimpse of the afterlife in the story of Elijah. Elijah is one of two men (the other is named Enoch) who was taken to heaven without dying. Probably because they didn't know any better, a group of prophets insists on hunting for Elijah—with no success!

Fifty men from the group of prophets followed them. The men stopped and stood not far away from them. They faced the place where Elijah and Elisha had stopped at the Jordan River. Elijah rolled up his coat. Then he struck the water with it. The water parted to the right and to the left. The two of them went across the river on dry ground.

After they had gone across, Elijah said to Elisha, "Tell me. What can I do for you before I'm taken away from you?"

"Please give me a double share of your spirit," Elisha replied.

"You have asked me for something that's very hard to do," Elijah said. "But suppose you see me when I'm taken away from you. Then you will receive what you have asked for. If you don't see me, you won't receive it."

They kept walking along and talking together. Suddenly there appeared a chariot and horses made of fire. The chariot and hors-

es came between the two men. Then Elijah went up to heaven in a strong wind. Elisha saw it and cried out to Elijah, "My father! You are like a father to me! You, Elijah, are the true chariots and horsemen of Israel!" Elisha didn't see Elijah anymore. Then Elisha took hold of his own garment and tore it in two.

He picked up the coat that had fallen from Elijah. He went back and stood on the bank of the Jordan River. Then he struck the water with Elijah's coat. "Where is the power of the LORD?" he asked. "Where is the power of the God of Elijah?" When Elisha struck the water, it parted to the right and to the left. He went across the river.

The group of prophets from Jericho were watching. They said, "The spirit of Elijah has been given to Elisha." They went over to Elisha. They bowed down to him with their faces toward the ground. "Look," they said. "We have 50 capable men. Let them go and look for your master. Perhaps the Spirit of the LORD has lifted him up. Maybe he has put him down on a mountain or in a valley."

"No," Elisha replied. "Don't send them."

But they kept asking until he felt he couldn't say no. So he said, "Send them." And they sent 50 men. They looked for Elijah for three days. But they didn't find him. So they returned to Elisha. He was staying in Jericho. Elisha said to them, "Didn't I tell you not to go?"   2 KINGS 2:7–18

Jesus Is Coming for Us

Elijah is the only person who was taken to heaven in a chariot of fire. For the rest of us, we will be taken to heaven by Jesus. Jesus told his disciples that he would return to earth. Whether we are alive when this happens, or whether we have already died, we will receive our spiritual bodies at this point. Those who have already died will be raised from the dead and will get new bodies. All believers from all time will be brought together and will be with Jesus forever. Let's read our key verse, where Jesus said...

"Do not let your hearts be troubled. You believe in God. Believe in me also. There are many rooms in my Father's house. If this were not true, would I have told you that I am going there? Would I have told you that I would prepare a place for you there? If I go and do that, I will come back. And I will take you to be with me. Then you will also be where I am." JOHN 14:1–3

A New Heaven and a New Earth

After Jesus returns and believers receive their spiritual bodies, there will be a final judgment by God where those who did not believe in God are sent to eternal punishment, and those who are children of God are brought into heaven.

Before the dazzling description of our future heavenly home, don't miss something special about the way we will be welcomed into heaven. A voice will announce that God will now live with us; we will be his people, and God will be our God. Amazingly, God used to say those exact words to the Israelites whenever he rescued them. He has wanted to be with his people for a long, long time, and our arrival in heaven will be the fulfillment of God's dream. What a happy day that will be!

I saw "a new heaven and a new earth." The first heaven and the first earth were completely gone. There was no longer any sea. I saw the Holy City, the new Jerusalem. It was coming down out of heaven from God. It was prepared like a bride beautifully dressed for her husband. I heard a loud voice from the throne. It said, "Look! God now makes his home with the people. He will live with them. They will be his people. And God himself will be with them and be their God. 'He will wipe away every tear from their eyes. There will be no more death.' And there will be no more sadness. There will be no more crying or pain. Things are no longer the way they used to be." REVELATION 21:1–4

The wall was made out of jasper. The city was made out of pure gold, as pure as glass. The foundations of the city walls were decorated with every kind of jewel. The first foundation was made out of jasper. The second was made out of sapphire. The third was made out of agate. The fourth was made out of emerald. The fifth was made out of onyx. The sixth was made out of ruby. The seventh was made out of chrysolite. The eighth was made

out of beryl. The ninth was made out of topaz. The tenth was made out of turquoise. The eleventh was made out of jacinth. The twelfth was made out of amethyst. The 12 gates were made from 12 pearls. Each gate was made out of a single pearl. The main street of the city was made out of gold. It was gold as pure as glass that people can see through clearly.

I didn't see a temple in the city. That's because the Lamb and the Lord God who rules over all are its temple. The city does not need the sun or moon to shine on it. God's glory is its light, and the Lamb is its lamp. The nations will walk by the light of the city. The kings of the world will bring their glory into it. Its gates will never be shut, because there will be no night there. The glory and honor of the nations will be brought into it. Only what is pure will enter the city. No one who causes people to believe lies will enter it. No one who does shameful things will enter it either. Only those whose names are written in the Lamb's book of life will enter the city.   REVELATION 21:18–27

Discussion Questions:

1. Going back to John's vision of what heaven will be like, hunt for these things: (1) the kind of person the Holy City will look like; (2) feelings we will not have in heaven; (3) the metal that won't look like metal; (4) five things that will not be in heaven.

2. What part of John's vision of the future seems the most exciting to you? Why?

3. If someone asked you how one can be sure of going to heaven, what would you say?

What Should I Do?

In a race all the runners run.
But only one gets the prize.
You know that, don't you?
So run in a way that will get you the prize.
All who take part in the games train hard.
They do it to get a crown that will not last.
But we do it to get a crown that will last forever.
1 Corinthians 9:24–25

God doesn't want us to stop at knowing about Jesus. He also wants us to follow Jesus' example — to *act* like Jesus. Learning to act like Jesus is a lot like training for a race — if you want to win the race and get the prize, you must practice! You don't win a race by talking about a race, dreaming about a race, or even knowing about races. In the verses above, Paul, one of the earliest followers of Jesus, says that if we want to win the best race of all and receive God's prize, we need to practice. And who better to imitate than Jesus, God's Son?

The next ten chapters are about the best ways to practice being like Jesus. If you put your heart into what you are about to read and practice what you learn, God will give you strength, even when it's tough. All these practices will help you love God and love other people better. If you want to act like Jesus, say:

I will...

1. Worship God for who he is and what he has done for me.
2. Pray to God to know him and find direction for my life.
3. Study the Bible to know God and his truth and to find direction for my daily life.
4. Focus on God and his priorities for my life.
5. Dedicate my life to God's plan.

6. Spend time with other Christians to accomplish God's plan in my life, in the lives of others and in the world.
7. Know my spiritual gifts and use them to bring about God's plan.
8. Offer my time to help God's plan.
9. Give my resources to help God's plan.
10. Share my faith with others to help God's plan.

On your mark ... get set ... GO!

Worship

O—π **KEY QUESTION:**
How do I honor God in the way he deserves?

O—π **KEY IDEA:**
I worship God for who he is and what he has done for me.

O—π **KEY VERSE:**
Come, let us sing for joy to the LORD.
Let us give a loud shout to the Rock who saves us.
Let us come to him and give him thanks.
Let us praise him with music and song.   *Psalm 95:1–2*

THINK ABOUT IT

Do you remember what the first commandment is? "Do not put any other gods in place of me." When we worship God, it helps us obey this commandment. Worship focuses our attention on God. We remember what we believe in our heads about God, and it helps us feel love for him in our hearts. When we worship we also feel him loving us back. Worship focuses us on God so we won't make other things more important in our lives than he is.

Worship Puts God First

Daniel was challenged to put a person in place of God. King Darius in the Old Testament was tricked into making a law that said everyone had to pray only to him for a month. Daniel's enemies knew he would never put anything before God, so they thought they had him trapped. Would Daniel worship King Darius? Would he make a god of his safety or his reputation

*and stop praying to God? Or would he put God first and keep
worshiping him?*

Daniel found out that the king had signed the order. In spite
of that, he did just as he had always done before. He went home
to his upstairs room. Its windows opened toward Jerusalem. He
went to his room three times a day to pray. He got down on his
knees and gave thanks to his God. Some of the other royal officials went to where Daniel was staying. They saw him praying
and asking God for help. So they went to the king. They spoke
to him about his royal order. They said, "Your Majesty, didn't
you sign an official order? It said that for the next 30 days your
people could pray only to you. They could not pray to anyone else,
whether god or human being. If they did, they would be thrown
into the lions' den."

The king answered, "The order must still be obeyed. It's what
the law of the Medes and Persians requires. So it can't be changed."

Then they spoke to the king again. They said, "Daniel is one
of the prisoners from Judah. He doesn't pay any attention to you,
Your Majesty. He doesn't obey the order you put in writing. He
still prays to his God three times a day." When the king heard
this, he was very upset. He didn't want Daniel to be harmed in
any way. Until sunset, he did everything he could to save him.

Then the men went as a group to King Darius. They said to
him, "Your Majesty, remember that no order or command you
give can be changed. That's what the law of the Medes and Persians requires."

So the king gave the order. Daniel was brought out and thrown
into the lions' den. The king said to him, "You always serve your
God faithfully. So may he save you!"

A stone was brought and placed over the opening of the den.
The king sealed it with his own special ring. He also sealed it with
the rings of his nobles. Then nothing could be done to help Daniel. The king returned to his palace. He didn't eat anything that
night. He didn't ask for anything to be brought to him for his
enjoyment. And he couldn't sleep.

As soon as the sun began to rise, the king got up. He hurried
to the lions' den. When he got near it, he called out to Daniel. His

voice was filled with great concern. He said, "Daniel! You serve the living God. You always serve him faithfully. So has he been able to save you from the lions?"

Daniel answered, "Your Majesty, may you live forever! My God sent his angel. And his angel shut the mouths of the lions. They haven't hurt me at all. That's because I haven't done anything wrong in God's sight. I've never done anything wrong to you either, Your Majesty."

The king was filled with joy. He ordered his servants to lift Daniel out of the den. So they did. They didn't see any wounds on him. That's because he had trusted in his God.

Then the king gave another order. The men who had said bad things about Daniel were brought in. They were thrown into the lions' den. So were their wives and children. Before they hit the bottom of the den, the lions attacked them. And the lions crushed all their bones.   DANIEL 6:10–24

Worship Reminds Us God Is in Control

Daniel worshiped God, not kings, not safety, and not his reputation. Daniel knew God was in control. Even when Daniel's circumstances changed, God was still in control of everything. We can worship God no matter where we are, no matter what is happening. In fact, when it feels like the worst time to worship God, that is often the best time because worship reminds us that God is in control. Paul and Silas in the New Testament even chose to worship God in jail.

The crowd joined the attack against Paul and Silas. The judges ordered that Paul and Silas be stripped and beaten with rods. They were whipped without mercy. Then they were thrown into prison. The jailer was commanded to guard them carefully. When he received these orders, he put Paul and Silas deep inside the prison. He fastened their feet so they couldn't get away.

About midnight Paul and Silas were praying. They were also singing hymns to God. The other prisoners were listening to them. Suddenly there was a powerful earthquake. It shook the prison from top to bottom. All at once the prison doors flew open. Everyone's chains came loose. The jailer woke up. He saw that the prison doors were open. He pulled out his sword and was going to kill himself. He thought the prisoners had escaped. "Don't harm yourself!" Paul shouted. "We are all here!"

The jailer called out for some lights. He rushed in, shaking with fear. He fell down in front of Paul and Silas. Then he brought them out. He asked, "Sirs, what must I do to be saved?"

They replied, "Believe in the Lord Jesus. Then you and everyone living in your house will be saved." They spoke the word of the Lord to him. They also spoke to all the others in his house. At that hour of the night, the jailer took Paul and Silas and washed their wounds. Right away he and everyone who lived with him were baptized. The jailer brought them into his house. He set a meal in front of them. He and everyone who lived with him were filled with joy. They had become believers in God.

Early in the morning the judges sent their officers to the jailer. They ordered him, "Let those men go."   ACTS 16:22–35

Communion Proclaims God's Love

We can see from Daniel's and Paul's examples that worshiping, even when it doesn't make sense, can affect those around

us. Sometimes people will decide to follow Jesus because they see us worshiping him. One way we can publicly worship Jesus is through communion. During communion, believers gather together to remember God's love for them and to publicly proclaim their love for him.

On the night the Lord Jesus was handed over to his enemies, he took bread. When he had given thanks, he broke it. He said, "This is my body. It is given for you. Every time you eat it, do it in memory of me." In the same way, after supper he took the cup. He said, "This cup is the new covenant in my blood. Every time you drink it, do it in memory of me." You eat the bread and drink the cup. When you do this, you are announcing the Lord's death until he comes again.   1 CORINTHIANS 11:23B–26

Discussion Questions:

1. What is your favorite way to worship God? Why is this your favorite?

2. Have you ever been kept from worshiping because something else was important or because you were having a rough time and didn't feel like it? How can worshiping anyway help you the next time that happens?

3. What does communion mean to you?

Prayer

KEY QUESTION:

How do I grow by communicating with God?

KEY IDEA:

I pray to God to know him and find direction for my life.

KEY VERSE:

If I had enjoyed having sin in my heart,
   the Lord would not have listened.
But God has surely listened.
   He has heard my prayer.
Give praise to God.
   He has accepted my prayer.
   He has not held back his love from me.   *Psalm 66:18–20*

THINK ABOUT IT

Worship and prayer are ways we communicate with God. When we talk to God in prayer, he wants us to be honest with him—he knows what we are thinking anyway! Pray about what bothers you and what you're excited about. Pray for answers to your questions and for power to do the things you don't feel you can. As our key verse says, "God has surely listened ... He has not held back his love from me!"

Jesus Needed to Pray

It was the most intense night of Jesus' life. He was facing a certain death and he knew it would be agony. So what did he do?

He prayed. If that's the tool Jesus used when facing the worst thing in his life, then we should turn to prayer too. But let's not pray like Jesus' friends in the next story! Prayer is the best thing for a friend who's in trouble, and Jesus certainly needed prayer on this night.

Then Jesus went with his disciples to a place called Gethsemane. He said to them, "Sit here while I go over there and pray." He took Peter and the two sons of Zebedee along with him. He began to be sad and troubled. Then he said to them, "My soul is very sad. I feel close to death. Stay here. Keep watch with me."

He went a little farther. Then he fell with his face to the ground. He prayed, "My Father, if it is possible, take this cup of suffering away from me. But let what you want be done, not what I want."

Then he returned to his disciples and found them sleeping. "Couldn't you men keep watch with me for one hour?" he asked Peter. "Watch and pray. Then you won't fall into sin when you are tempted. The spirit is willing, but the body is weak."

Jesus went away a second time. He prayed, "My Father, is it possible for this cup to be taken away? But if I must drink it, may what you want be done."

Then he came back. Again he found them sleeping. They couldn't keep their eyes open. So he left them and went away once more. For the third time he prayed the same thing.

Then he returned to the disciples. He said to them, "Are you still sleeping and resting? Look! The hour has come. The Son of Man is about to be handed over to sinners. Get up! Let us go! Here comes the one who is handing me over to them!"

MATTHEW 26:36–46

Jesus Taught Us to Pray

Long before this, Jesus' disciples asked him to teach them how to pray. He responded with an example we call the Lord's Prayer. Jesus encourages us to ask, search, and knock when we pray.

One day Jesus was praying in a certain place. When he finished, one of his disciples spoke to him. "Lord," he said, "teach us to pray, just as John taught his disciples."

Jesus said to them, "When you pray, this is what you should say.

> "'Father,
> may your name be honored.
> May your kingdom come.
> Give us each day our daily bread.
> Forgive us our sins,
>   as we also forgive everyone who sins against us.
> Keep us from falling into sin when we are tempted.'"

LUKE 11:1–4

"So here is what I say to you. Ask, and it will be given to you. Search, and you will find. Knock, and the door will be opened to you. Everyone who asks will receive. The one who searches will find. And the door will be opened to the one who knocks."

LUKE 11:9–10

Paul told us to turn our worries into prayers and to not forget to thank God too!

Don't worry about anything. No matter what happens, tell God about everything. Ask and pray, and give thanks to him.

PHILIPPIANS 4:6

Asking God for Direction

Throughout the Bible, we find people praying for guidance. We want God to direct our steps, but sometimes we are not sure what he wants us to do, so we need to ask. In the Old Testament, God told a man named Gideon to lead the Israelites in battle. Gideon was surprised by this assignment. He asked God about what God was asking him to do. When we take our questions to God, he will provide the answers we need!

The LORD turned to Gideon. He said to him, "You are strong. Go and save Israel from the power of Midian. I am sending you."

"Pardon me, sir," Gideon replied, "but how can I possibly save Israel? My family group is the weakest in the tribe of Manasseh. And I'm the least important member of my family."

The LORD answered, "I will be with you. So you will strike down the Midianites. You will leave no one alive." JUDGES 6:14–16

Gideon said to God, "You promised you would use me to save Israel. Please do something for me. I'll put a piece of wool on the threshing floor. Suppose dew is only on the wool tomorrow morning. And suppose the ground all around it is dry. Then I will know that you will use me to save Israel. I'll know that your promise will come true." And that's what happened. Gideon got up early the next day. He squeezed the dew out of the wool. The water filled a bowl.

Then Gideon said to God, "Don't be angry with me. Let me ask you for just one more thing. Let me use the wool for one more test. But this time make the wool dry. And let the ground be covered with dew." So that night God did it. Only the wool was dry. The ground all around it was covered with dew. JUDGES 6:36–40

The Lord told Gideon he had too many men for this battle. God whittled down his fighting force from 22,000 men to 300, so that when they won the battle, they would have to say the Lord won the battle for them.

The LORD spoke to Gideon. He said, "With the help of the 300 men who lapped up the water I will save you. I will hand the Midianites over to you. Let all the other men go home." So Gideon sent those Israelites home. But he kept the 300 men. They took over the supplies and trumpets the others had left.   JUDGES 7:7–8A

"Watch me," he told them. "Do what I do. I'll go to the edge of the enemy camp. Then do exactly as I do. I and everyone with me will blow our trumpets. Then blow your trumpets from your positions all around the camp. And shout the battle cry, 'For the LORD and for Gideon!'"

Gideon and the 100 men with him reached the edge of the enemy camp. It was about ten o'clock at night. It was just after the guard had been changed. Gideon and his men blew their trumpets. They broke the jars that were in their hands. The three fighting groups blew their trumpets. They smashed their jars. They held their torches in their left hands. They held in their right hands the trumpets they were going to blow. Then they shouted the battle cry, "A sword for the LORD and for Gideon!" Each man stayed in his position around the camp. But all the Midianites ran away in fear. They were crying out as they ran.

When the 300 trumpets were blown, the LORD caused all the men in the enemy camp to start fighting one another. They attacked one another with their swords. The army ran away.

JUDGES 7:17–22A

Discussion Questions:

1. Divide the Lord's Prayer into three parts by writing these headings next to the line or lines they fit with: (1) Putting God First, (2) Asking for What We Need, and (3) Asking for Help to Live Right. Which of these do you pray most often? Which do you need to pray more?

2. Do you find it easy to tell God about everything, as it says in Philippians 4:6? Or are some things harder for you to pray about?

3. What part of Gideon's story do you find the most surprising? Why?

Bible Study

⊙━π KEY QUESTION:
How do I study God's Word?

⊙━π KEY IDEA:
I study the Bible to know God and his truth and to find direction for my daily life.

⊙━π KEY VERSE:
The word of God is alive and active. It is sharper than any sword that has two edges. It cuts deep enough to separate soul from spirit. It can separate bones from joints. It judges the thoughts and purposes of the heart. *Hebrews 4:12*

THINK ABOUT IT

The Bible is the actual Word of God, given to us by our good God. The ancient stories and words are "alive and active" and capable of leading us down the right path. But like a trustworthy map, we must study it in order for it to help us get to where God wants to take us.

The Key to Success

After Moses died, God put Joshua in charge of the Israelites. This was a big job, and he told Joshua to be strong and brave. Then he told Joshua what would be the key to his success. In fact, he told him if he did this, he would have success wherever he would go. What was this amazing key to success? Underline the answer when you find it.

"Joshua, no one will be able to oppose you as long as you live. I will be with you, just as I was with Moses. I will never leave you. I will never desert you. Be strong and brave. You will lead these people. They will take the land as their very own. It is the land I promised to give their people of long ago.

"Be strong and very brave. Make sure you obey the whole law my servant Moses gave you. Do not turn away from it to the right or the left. Then you will have success everywhere you go. Never stop reading this Book of the Law. Day and night you must think about what it says. Make sure you do everything written in it. Then things will go well with you. And you will have great success. Here is what I am commanding you to do. Be strong and brave. Do not be afraid. Do not lose hope. I am the LORD your God. I will be with you everywhere you go."   JOSHUA 1:5–9

How to Study the Bible

God told Joshua to think about his Word day and night. He told him to "do everything written in it." That's a tall order! It's interesting that the longest chapter in the Bible, Psalm 119, is entirely devoted to the subject of God's Word. This psalm is all about loving, knowing and following God's Word. See how many ways you can find to study and love the Bible in these verses.

How can a young person keep their life pure?
By living according to your word.

I trust in you with all my heart.
    Don't let me wander away from your commands.
I have hidden your word in my heart
    so that I won't sin against you.   Psalm 119:9 –11

I spend time thinking about your rules.
    I consider how you want me to live.
I take delight in your orders.
    I won't fail to obey your word.   Psalm 119:15 –16

Open my eyes so that I can see
    the wonderful truths in your law.   Psalm 119:18

Teach me to live as you command,
    because that makes me very happy.
Make me want to follow your covenant laws
    instead of wanting to gain things only for myself.
       Psalm 119:35–36

Your word is like a lamp that shows me the way.
    It is like a light that guides me.   Psalm 119:105

How to Understand the Bible

The Bible is no ordinary book. It will help us and change us, but only if we let it. In the New Testament, Jesus taught that the condition of our hearts is important when we hear or read God's Word. We have to be open to God's message in order to hear it and understand it. If you are having trouble understanding what you read, it might be a heart problem, not a head problem!

Jesus left the house and sat by the Sea of Galilee. Large crowds gathered around him. So he got into a boat and sat down. All the people stood on the shore. Then he told them many things using stories. He said, "A farmer went out to plant his seed. He scattered the seed on the ground. Some fell on a path. Birds came and ate it up. Some seed fell on rocky places, where there wasn't much soil. The plants came up quickly, because the soil wasn't

deep. When the sun came up, it burned the plants. They dried up because they had no roots. Other seed fell among thorns. The thorns grew up and crowded out the plants. Still other seed fell on good soil. It produced a crop 100, 60 or 30 times more than what was planted. Whoever has ears should listen."

The disciples came to him. They asked, "Why do you use stories when you speak to the people?"

He replied, "Because you have been given the knowledge of the secrets of the kingdom of heaven. It has not been given to outsiders. Everyone who has this kind of knowledge will be given more knowledge. In fact, they will have very much. If anyone doesn't have this kind of knowledge, even what little they have will be taken away from them. Here is why I use stories when I speak to the people. I say,

> "They look, but they don't really see.
> They listen, but they don't really hear or understand.

In them the words of the prophet Isaiah come true. He said,

> " 'You will hear but never understand.
> You will see but never know what you are seeing.
> The hearts of these people have become stubborn.
> They can barely hear with their ears.
> They have closed their eyes.
> Otherwise they might see with their eyes.
> They might hear with their ears.
> They might understand with their hearts.
> They might turn to the Lord, and then he would heal
> them.'

But blessed are your eyes because they see. And blessed are your ears because they hear. What I'm about to tell you is true. Many prophets and godly people wanted to see what you see. But they didn't see it. They wanted to hear what you hear. But they didn't hear it.

"Listen! Here is the meaning of the story of the farmer. People hear the message about the kingdom but do not understand it. Then the evil one comes. He steals what was planted in their hearts. Those people are like the seed planted on a path. The seed that fell on rocky places is like other people. They hear the message and at once receive it with joy. But they have no roots. So they last only a short time. They quickly fall away from the faith when trouble or suffering comes because of the message. The seed that fell among the thorns is like others who hear the message. But then the worries of this life and the false promises of wealth crowd it out. They keep the message from producing fruit. But the seed that fell on good soil is like those who hear the message and understand it. They produce a crop 100, 60 or 30 times more than the farmer planted."   MATTHEW 13:1–23

Discussion Questions:

1. Our key verse says God's Word is like a sword. Why is it like a sword? Has God's Word ever been like a sword in your life? When?

2. In contrast, Psalm 119:105 says God's Word is like a lamp. Why is that a good way to describe the Bible? When has God's Word been like a lamp in your life?

3. According to Psalm 119:11, why is it important to memorize God's Word (hide his Word in your heart)? If you are not memorizing God's Word yet, start by memorizing Psalm 119:11!

14

Single-Mindedness

🗝 **KEY QUESTION:**
How to I keep my focus on Jesus?

🗝 **KEY IDEA:**
I focus on God and his priorities for my life.

🗝 **KEY VERSE:**
Put God's kingdom first. Do what he wants you to do.
Then all those things will also be given to you.

Matthew 6:33

THINK ABOUT IT

We have learned about ways to communicate with God through worship, prayer, and Bible study. Now we turn our attention to how God wants us to arrange our lives—he wants us to be single-minded. The term single-minded means just what it sounds like: having a mind that is focused on one single thing. Sometimes we use the word "priorities" instead: when we're single-minded we have strong priorities. We know what is most important in our lives, and we arrange our lives around that priority. God wants us to stay focused on him, especially when other priorities try to overtake us.

King Jehoshaphat Stays Focused on God

Let's journey back in time to the Old Testament land of Judah. King Jehoshaphat is about to hear some terrible news. The way he leads his people in the crisis shows us how single-mindedness pays off.

The bad news: three armies are marching toward Judah.

The Moabites, Ammonites and some Meunites went to war against Jehoshaphat.   2 CHRONICLES 20:1

The good news: the king's first action is to fast (go without food) and pray.

Jehoshaphat was alarmed. So he decided to ask the LORD for advice. He told all the people of Judah to go without eating. The people came together to ask the LORD for help. In fact, they came from every town in Judah to pray to him.   2 CHRONICLES 20:3–4

At the end of Jehoshaphat's prayer, he declares his single-minded focus on God for help. Notice that he is not trying to solve this problem himself by doing things like building walls, gathering his army, or making weapons.

"Our God, won't you please judge them? We don't have the power to face this huge army that's attacking us. We don't know what to do. But we're looking to you to help us."   2 CHRONICLES 20:12

A prophet tells the king he doesn't have to fight this battle, because "the battle is not yours, it is God's." Jehoshaphat and all the people immediately trusted themselves to God, and they worshiped him and sang praises.

Jahaziel said, "King Jehoshaphat, listen! All you who live in Judah and Jerusalem, listen! The LORD says to you, 'Do not be afraid. Do not lose hope because of this huge army. The battle is not yours. It is God's."   2 CHRONICLES 20:15

"'You will not have to fight this battle. Take your positions. Stand firm. You will see how the LORD will save you. Judah and Jerusalem, do not be afraid. Do not lose hope. Go out and face them tomorrow. The LORD will be with you.'"

Jehoshaphat bowed down with his face toward the ground. All the people of Judah and Jerusalem also bowed down. They worshiped the LORD. Then some Levites from the families of Kohath

and Korah stood up. They praised the Lord, the God of Israel. They praised him with very loud voices.   2 Chronicles 20:17–19

The people of Judah did not prepare for battle in the typical way. Because they had faith in God's message to them that they would not fight this battle, they put the praise and worship team in front of the army and marched to the battlefield led by the singers. That must have been the most unusual battle formation in history!

Early in the morning all the people left for the Desert of Tekoa. As they started out, Jehoshaphat stood up. He said, "Judah, listen to me! People of Jerusalem, listen to me! Have faith in the Lord your God. He'll take good care of you. Have faith in his prophets. Then you will have success." Jehoshaphat asked the people for advice. Then he appointed men to sing to the Lord. He wanted them to praise the Lord because of his glory and holiness. They marched out in front of the army. They said,

"Give thanks to the LORD.
   His faithful love continues forever."

They began to sing and praise him.   2 CHRONICLES 20:20–22A

*True to his promise, God made the three enemy armies attack
and destroy each other. The people of Judah never shot one
arrow or lifted one sword. All they had to do was stand on a hill
and watch, then collect all the valuables.*

The Ammonites and Moabites rose up against the men from
Mount Seir. They destroyed them. They put an end to them.
When they finished killing the men from Seir, they destroyed one
another.

The men of Judah came to the place that looks out over the
desert. They turned to look down at the huge army. But all they
saw was dead bodies lying there on the ground. No one had escaped. So Jehoshaphat and his men went down there to carry
off anything of value. Among the dead bodies they found a large
amount of supplies, clothes and other things of value. There was
more than they could take away. There was so much it took three
days to collect all of it. On the fourth day they gathered together
in the Valley of Berakah. There they praised the LORD. That's why
it's called the Valley of Berakah to this day.   2 CHRONICLES 20:23–26

*The word "berakah" means "praise." The men of Judah
returned to Jerusalem the way they left—led by the singers,
praising and thanking God. They never lost their single-minded
focus on God, and God rewarded them.*

Then all the men of Judah and Jerusalem returned to Jerusalem. They were filled with joy. Jehoshaphat led them. The LORD
had made them happy because all their enemies were dead. They
entered Jerusalem and went to the LORD's temple. They were
playing harps, lyres and trumpets.

All the surrounding kingdoms began to have respect for God.
They had heard how the LORD had fought against Israel's enemies. The kingdom of Jehoshaphat was at peace. His God had
given him peace and rest on every side.   2 CHRONICLES 20:27–30

Peter Loses Focus on Jesus

Jehoshaphat kept his eyes on God, and God took good care of him. When we keep our eyes on Jesus, God will take good care of us too. It's important that we don't take our eyes off Jesus, even for a second. Let's take a look at Peter. He had faith, but when he looked away from Jesus, he got into some trouble.

Shortly before dawn, Jesus went out to the disciples. He walked on the lake. They saw him walking on the lake and were terrified. "It's a ghost!" they said. And they cried out in fear.

Right away Jesus called out to them, "Be brave! It is I. Don't be afraid."

"Lord, is it you?" Peter asked. "If it is, tell me to come to you on the water."

"Come," Jesus said.

So Peter got out of the boat. He walked on the water toward Jesus. But when Peter saw the wind, he was afraid. He began to sink. He cried out, "Lord! Save me!"

Right away Jesus reached out his hand and caught him. "Your faith is so small!" he said. "Why did you doubt me?"

When they climbed into the boat, the wind died down. Then those in the boat worshiped Jesus. They said, "You really are the Son of God!"   MATTHEW 14:25–33

Discussion Questions:

1. Compare Jehoshaphat's story with the three phrases in our key verse. How did the king put God's kingdom first? How did he do what God wanted him to do? How did the last line of the verse come true? What do you think "all those things" refers to in the life of a Christian?

2. When you get bad news, what is your first reaction? Do you immediately pray, or do you have another way of handling pressure?

3. Put yourself in Peter's position. Would you have dared to climb out of the boat? Would you have had faith to walk on the water? Would you have taken your eyes off Jesus?

Total Surrender

THINK ABOUT IT

When you decide to follow Jesus, you give your life to him. You say, "Jesus, I make you the ruler of my life. I will let you be in charge." That's what happens when we surrender: we let go of our right to run our lives and we let God take over. That means we've got to believe that God can do a better job at taking care of us than we can. Even when it seems like we could get hurt, total surrender trusts God all the way.

"Even if God does not save us, we will not serve your gods!"

King Nebuchadnezzar made a 90-foot statue of gold. That's as tall as a nine-story building! He commanded that everyone had to bow down and worship the statue. If they didn't, their punishment would be severe—they would be burned alive in a furnace. Some people noticed that Shadrach, Meshach and Abednego did not bow like everyone else. So, they told on them! Nebuchadnezzar was very angry, but he gave them one more chance ... worship the statue, or be thrown into the furnace.

Shadrach, Meshach and Abednego replied to him. They said, "King Nebuchadnezzar, we don't need to talk about this anymore. We might be thrown into the blazing furnace. But the God we serve is able to bring us out of it alive. He will save us from your power. But we want you to know this, Your Majesty. Even if we knew that our God wouldn't save us, we still wouldn't serve your gods. We wouldn't worship the gold statue you set up."

Then Nebuchadnezzar was very angry with Shadrach, Meshach and Abednego. The look on his face changed. And he ordered that the furnace be heated seven times hotter than usual. He also gave some of the strongest soldiers in his army a command. He ordered them to tie up Shadrach, Meshach and Abednego. Then he told his men to throw them into the blazing furnace. So they were tied up. Then they were thrown into the furnace. They were wearing their robes, pants, turbans and other clothes. The king's command was carried out quickly. The furnace was so hot that its flames killed the soldiers who threw Shadrach, Meshach and Abednego into it. So the three men were firmly tied up. And they fell into the blazing furnace.

Then King Nebuchadnezzar leaped to his feet. He was so amazed he asked his advisers, "Didn't we tie up three men? Didn't we throw three men into the fire?"

They replied, "Yes, we did, Your Majesty."

The king said, "Look! I see four men walking around in the fire. They aren't tied up. And the fire hasn't even harmed them. The fourth man looks like a son of the gods."

Then the king approached the opening of the blazing furnace. He shouted, "Shadrach, Meshach and Abednego, come out! You who serve the Most High God, come here!"

So they came out of the fire. The royal rulers, high officials, governors and advisers crowded around them. They saw that the fire hadn't harmed their bodies. Not one hair on their heads was burned. Their robes weren't burned either. And they didn't even smell like smoke.

Then Nebuchadnezzar said, "May the God of Shadrach, Meshach and Abednego be praised! He has sent his angel and saved his servants. They trusted in him. They refused to obey my command. They were willing to give up their lives. They would rather die than serve or worship any god except their own God."

DANIEL 3:16–28

"If I have to die, I'll die!"

Another Old Testament story of total surrender is the story of Esther. Esther and her cousin Mordecai were Jews living under the rule of the Persian king Xerxes. King Xerxes chose Esther to be his queen, but he didn't know that she was a Jew. One of the king's men, Haman, hated Mordecai because he refused to bow down and honor Haman. Haman set up a date to kill all the Jews, and Mordecai with them. Mordecai sent a messenger named Hathak to Esther to ask her to try to stop this wicked plan. Esther had a choice to make. She could try to protect herself and her position as queen, or she could try to save the Jews, risking her own life in the process. Like Shadrach, Meshach and Abednego, Esther chose total surrender.

Mordecai told [Hathak] to tell [Esther] to go and beg the king for mercy. Mordecai wanted her to make an appeal to the king for her people.

Hathak went back and reported to Esther what Mordecai had said. Then Esther directed him to give an answer to Mordecai. She told him to say, "There is a certain law that everyone knows about. All the king's officials know about it. The people in the royal territories know about it. It applies to any man or woman who approaches the king in the inner courtyard without being sent for. It says they must be put to death. But there is a way out. Suppose the king reaches out his gold scepter toward them. Then their lives will be spared. But 30 days have gone by since the king sent for me."

Esther's words were reported to Mordecai. Then he sent back an answer. He said, "You live in the king's palace. But don't think that just because you are there you will be the only Jew who will escape. What if you don't say anything at this time? Then help for the Jews will come from another place. But you and your family will die. Who knows? It's possible that you became queen for a time just like this."

Then Esther sent a reply to Mordecai. She said, "Go. Gather together all the Jews who are in Susa. And fast for my benefit. Don't eat or drink anything for three days. Don't do it night or day. I and my attendants will fast just as you do. Then I'll go to the king. I'll do it even though it's against the law. And if I have to die, I'll die." ESTHER 4:8B –16

After they all had fasted, Esther approached the king, and he reached out his gold scepter to her, sparing her life. Eventually Esther was able to save the Jews by telling the king about Haman's plan.

"Look! I see heaven open!"

In the New Testament, Stephen was brought before the Jew-ish leaders because they did not like what he was saying about Jesus. They found people to lie about Stephen so they would have an excuse to kill him. But at his trial he had one last chance to speak in his own defense. Instead of trying to save himself, he spoke boldly about Jesus. Read what happens as he gets to the end of his speech. Stephen was saying . . .

"You stubborn people! You won't obey! You won't listen! You are just like your people of long ago! You always oppose the Holy Spirit! Was there ever a prophet your people didn't try to hurt? They even killed those who told about the coming of the Blame-less One. And now you have handed him over to his enemies. You have murdered him. The law you received was given by angels. But you haven't obeyed it."

When the members of the Sanhedrin heard this, they became very angry. They were so angry they ground their teeth at Ste-phen. But he was full of the Holy Spirit. He looked up to heaven and saw God's glory. He saw Jesus standing at God's right hand. "Look!" he said. "I see heaven open. The Son of Man is standing at God's right hand."

When the Sanhedrin heard this, they covered their ears. They yelled at the top of their voices. They all rushed at him. They dragged him out of the city. They began to throw stones at him to kill him. The people who had brought false charges against Ste-phen took off their coats. They placed them at the feet of a young man named Saul.

While the members of the Sanhedrin were throwing stones at Stephen, he prayed. "Lord Jesus, receive my spirit," he said. Then he fell on his knees. He cried out, "Lord! Don't hold this sin against them!" When he had said this, he died.   ACTS 7:51–60

Discussion Questions:

1. What are some similarities between the three stories in this chapter? What are some of the character qualities you saw in the people in these stories?

2. Our key verse says when we offer our bodies to God, we are worshiping him in the right way. How did the people in our three stories offer their bodies to God? How did it show their worship of God?

3. Is there anything in your life you have not given to God to take charge of? What is keeping you from total surrender?

Biblical Community

⊶ⁿ **KEY QUESTION:**
How do I develop healthy relationships with others?

⊶ⁿ **KEY IDEA:**
I spend time with other Christians to accomplish God's plan in my life, in the lives of others and in the world.

⊶ⁿ **KEY VERSE:**
All the believers were together. They shared everything they had. They sold property and other things they owned. They gave to anyone who needed something. Every day they met together in the temple courtyard. They ate meals together in their homes. Their hearts were glad and sincere. They praised God. They were respected by all the people. Every day the Lord added to their group those who were being saved.   *Acts 2:44–47*

THINK ABOUT IT

From the beginning God made us for community. The Trinity was the first community. Then God made Adam and Eve so he could be in community with them. He built the church, a community of Christians. God obviously wants us to be connected to him and to each other. But biblical community means more than just a group of people who share something in common. When we are in a biblical community, we have a strong bond with each other, we work together for a common goal, and we take care of each other.

Working Together

We see an example of a strong bond between God's people in the Old Testament account of Nehemiah. At one sad point in Israel's history, the wall around Jerusalem was destroyed. Nehemiah surveyed the wall to see how damaged it was. Then he rallied the community to help him rebuild. Not everyone wanted the wall built. Some made fun of them to try to get them to stop. But the community banded together and showed the nations around them what can be accomplished when people work together for God. Nehemiah wrote:

I went to Jerusalem and stayed there for three days. Then at night I took a few other people with me to check out the walls. I hadn't told anyone what my God wanted me to do for Jerusalem. There weren't any donkeys with me except the one I was riding on.

That night I went out through the Valley Gate. I went toward the Jackal Well and the Dung Gate. I checked out the walls of Jerusalem. They had been broken down. I also checked the city gates. Fire had burned them up. I moved on toward the Fountain Gate and the King's Pool. But there wasn't enough room for my donkey to get through. It was still night. I went up the Kidron Valley. I kept checking the wall. Finally, I turned back. I went back in through the Valley Gate. The officials didn't know where I had gone or what I had done. That's because I hadn't said anything to anyone yet. I hadn't told the priests or nobles or officials. And I hadn't spoken to any other Jews who would be rebuilding the wall.

I said to them, "You can see the trouble we're in. Jerusalem has been destroyed. Fire has burned up its gates. Come on. Let's rebuild the wall of Jerusalem. Then people won't be ashamed anymore." I also told them how my gracious God was helping me. And I told them what the king had said to me.

They replied, "Let's start rebuilding." So they began that good work.

But Sanballat, the Horonite, heard about it. So did Tobiah, the official from Ammon. Geshem, the Arab, heard about it too. All of them laughed at us. They made fun of us. "What do you think you are doing?" they asked. "Are you turning against the king?"

I answered, "The God of heaven will give us success. We serve him. So we'll start rebuilding the walls. But you don't have any share in Jerusalem. You don't have any claim to it. You don't have any right to worship here."

Eliashib the high priest and the other priests went to work. They rebuilt the Sheep Gate. They set it apart to God. They put its doors in place. They continued to rebuild the wall up to the Tower of the Hundred. They set the tower apart to God. Then they continued to rebuild the wall all the way to the Tower of Hananel. Some men from Jericho rebuilt the next part of the wall. And Zakkur rebuilt the next part. He was the son of Imri.

NEHEMIAH 2:11—3:2

Nehemiah went on to describe how dozens of families worked together to rebuild the different sections of the wall.

So the city wall was completed on the 25th day of the month of Elul. It was finished in 52 days. NEHEMIAH 6:15

Sharing Together

In the New Testament where the text of our key verse is found, we read that when the church was just starting, the believers "shared their lives together." Imagine if we were to live like that today. We would enjoy a biblical community where we help each other, enjoy fellowship with each other, love each other, and take care of each other. There might not be any more needy people if we all lived as a biblical community!

The believers studied what the apostles taught. They shared their lives together. They ate and prayed together. Everyone was amazed at what God was doing. They were amazed when the apostles performed many wonders and signs. All the believers were together. They shared everything they had. They sold property and other things they owned. They gave to anyone who needed something. Every day they met together in the temple courtyard. They ate meals together in their homes. Their hearts were glad and sincere. They praised God. They were respected by all the people. Every day the Lord added to their group those who were being saved.   ACTS 2:42–47

All the believers were agreed in heart and mind. They didn't claim that anything they had was their own. Instead, they shared everything they owned. With great power the apostles continued their teaching. They were telling people that the Lord Jesus had risen from the dead. And God's grace was working powerfully in all of them. So there were no needy persons among them. From time to time, those who owned land or houses sold them. They brought the money from the sales. They put it down at the apostles' feet. It was then given out to anyone who needed it.

Joseph was a Levite from Cyprus. The apostles called him Barnabas. The name Barnabas means Son of Help. Barnabas sold a field he owned. He brought the money from the sale. He put it down at the apostles' feet.   ACTS 4:32–37

We know what love is because Jesus Christ gave his life for us. So we should give our lives for our brothers and sisters. Suppose someone sees a brother or sister in need and is able to help them.

And suppose that person doesn't take pity on these needy people. Then how can the love of God be in that person? **Dear children, don't just talk about love. Put your love into action. Then it will truly be love.**   1 JOHN 3:16–18

Discussion Questions:

1. Nehemiah saw a big problem, and he invited people to help him solve it. Have you ever been part of accomplishing something with a group which you never could have done alone? How did it feel?

2. Our key verse, Acts 2:44–47, describes a wonderful biblical community. When people saw biblical community in action, how did they respond? What was it about biblical community that caused this reaction?

3. Re-read the verses in the "Sharing Together" section. Circle the words that describe how the people lived in biblical community. Put a star next to the word or phrase that sounds most appealing to you. Why are you drawn to it?

Spiritual Gifts

🔑 **KEY QUESTION:**
What gifts and skills has God given me to serve others?

🔑 **KEY IDEA:**
I know my spiritual gifts and use them to bring about God's plan.

🔑 **KEY VERSE:**
Each of us has one body with many parts. And the parts do not all have the same purpose. So also we are many persons. But in Christ we are one body. And each part of the body belongs to all the other parts. We all have gifts. They differ according to the grace God has given to each of us.   *Romans 12:4–6a*

THINK ABOUT IT

Our biblical community is also known as the body of Christ. As our key verse says, a body has many parts that are all needed by the whole body, as does the body of Christ. We each have a spiritual purpose, or gift, that the Holy Spirit gave us that is needed by the rest of the body. If we don't use our gift to serve others, the whole body suffers.

Spiritual Gifts in the Old Testament

Spiritual gifts are special abilities given by the Holy Spirit. They are meant to be used by God's people to complete God's work. Although the term "spiritual gift" isn't found in the Old Testament, we see the Holy Spirit working through people during this time. For example, the Holy Spirit gave Daniel the ability to

understand the meaning of a complicated dream, which God
used as a way to reveal his power to King Nebuchadnezzar.

In the second year of Nebuchadnezzar's rule, he had a dream.
His mind was troubled. He couldn't sleep. So the king sent for
those who claimed to get knowledge by using magic. He also sent
for those who practiced evil magic and those who studied the
heavens. He wanted them to tell him what he had dreamed. They
came in and stood in front of the king. He said to them, "I had a
dream. It troubles me. So I want to know what it means."

Then those who studied the heavens answered the king. They
spoke in Aramaic. They said, "King Nebuchadnezzar, may you
live forever! Tell us what you dreamed. Then we'll explain what
it means."

The king replied to them, "I have made up my mind. You must
tell me what I dreamed. And you must tell me what it means. If
you don't, I'll have you cut to pieces. And I'll have your houses
turned into piles of trash."   Daniel 2:1–5

The magicians were dismayed. No one had ever asked for such
a thing, and no human being they knew of could perform such
a thing. But when they said this to King Nebuchadnezzar, it
made him so angry he ordered to have all of his wise men put
to death. When an official named Arioch told Daniel what was
happening, Daniel respectfully asked if he could have time to
interpret the dream for the king. Then he and his friends prayed
together that God would reveal the mystery of the dream to
him, and God answered their prayers.

So Arioch took Daniel to the king at once. Arioch said, "I have
found a man among those you brought here from Judah. He can
tell you what your dream means."

Nebuchadnezzar spoke to Daniel, who was also called Bel-
teshazzar. The king asked him, "Are you able to tell me what I saw
in my dream? And can you tell me what it means?"

Daniel replied, "You have asked us to explain a mystery to you.
But no wise man can do that. And those who try to figure things
out by using magic can't do it either. But there is a God in heaven

who can explain mysteries. King Nebuchadnezzar, he has shown you what is going to happen. Here is what you dreamed while lying in bed. And here are the visions that passed through your mind.   DANIEL 2:25–28

"King Nebuchadnezzar, you looked up and saw a large statue standing in front of you. It was huge. It shone brightly. And it terrified you. The head of the statue was made out of pure gold. Its chest and arms were made out of silver. Its stomach and thighs were made out of bronze. Its legs were made out of iron. And its feet were partly iron and partly baked clay. While you were watching, a rock was cut out. But human hands didn't do it. It struck the statue on its feet of iron and clay. It smashed them. Then the iron and clay were broken to pieces. So were the bronze, silver and gold. All of them were broken to pieces. They became like straw on a threshing floor at harvest time. The wind blew them away without leaving a trace. But the rock that struck the statue became a huge mountain. It filled the whole earth."

DANIEL 2:31–35

Daniel then told the king what his dream meant. He, King Nebuchadnezzar, was the head of gold, the greatest king of all. After him, less and less powerful kingdoms would take over, signified by the arms of silver, the stomach of bronze, the legs of iron. The last kingdom would crush and break all the others. Then God would set up a kingdom that could never be destroyed, never be taken over, and would last forever. Daniel finished by saying again that it was God, not he, who gave this interpretation of the king's dream to him.

"The great God has shown you what will take place in days to come. The dream is true. And you can trust the meaning of it that I have explained to you."

Then King Nebuchadnezzar bowed low in front of Daniel. He wanted to honor him. So he ordered that an offering and incense be offered up to him. The king said to Daniel, "I'm sure your God is the greatest God of all. He is the Lord of kings. He explains mysteries. That's why you were able to explain the mystery of my dream."   DANIEL 2:45B–47

The Holy Spirit in Us

In the Old Testament, the Holy Spirit came on special occasions to give power to certain people for specific situations. Today, believers have it even better. When we decide to follow Jesus, the Holy Spirit comes to live in us for the rest of our lives! And he gives each of us important spiritual gifts that are all necessary and useful for serving God.

The Holy Spirit is given to each of us in a special way. That is for the good of all. To some people the Spirit gives a message of wisdom. To others the same Spirit gives a message of knowledge. To others the same Spirit gives faith. To others that one Spirit gives gifts of healing. To others he gives the power to do miracles. To others he gives the ability to prophesy. To others he gives the ability to tell the spirits apart. To others he gives the ability to speak in different kinds of languages they had not known before. And to still others he gives the ability to explain what was said in those languages. All the gifts are produced by one and the same Spirit. He gives gifts to each person, just as he decides.

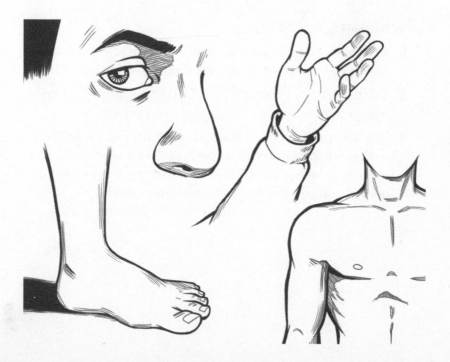

There is one body, but it has many parts. But all its many parts make up one body. It is the same with Christ. We were all baptized by one Holy Spirit. And so we are formed into one body. It didn't matter whether we were Jews or Gentiles, slaves or free people. We were all given the same Spirit to drink. So the body is not made up of just one part. It has many parts.

Suppose the foot says, "I am not a hand. So I don't belong to the body." By saying this, it cannot stop being part of the body. And suppose the ear says, "I am not an eye. So I don't belong to the body." By saying this, it cannot stop being part of the body. If the whole body were an eye, how could it hear? If the whole body were an ear, how could it smell? God has placed each part in the body just as he wanted it to be. If all the parts were the same, how could there be a body? As it is, there are many parts. But there is only one body.

The eye can't say to the hand, "I don't need you!" The head can't say to the feet, "I don't need you!" In fact, it is just the opposite. The parts of the body that seem to be weaker are the ones we can't do without.   1 Corinthians 12:7–22

Discussion Questions:

1. Why was it important that Daniel tell King Nebuchadnezzar where his spiritual gift came from?

2. What spiritual gift or gifts has God given you? What are some ways you can use your gifts to serve God?

3. Was there a time when you had an injury, even a small one, and it affected your whole body? Thinking about that, why does the body of Christ need you to use your spiritual gift, even if you think it's not very important?

Offering My Time

🔑 KEY QUESTION:
How do I best use my time to serve God and others?

🔑 KEY IDEA:
I offer my time to help God's plan.

🔑 KEY VERSE:
Do everything you say or do in the name of the Lord Jesus. Always give thanks to God the Father through Christ.

Colossians 3:17

THINK ABOUT IT

When we think about what we can give to God, we may think about our money or our spiritual gifts. But we might not think about giving God our time. The minutes in our day are just as important as the dollars in our wallet. God wants to be our first priority on our calendar.

It Does Not Pay to Be Slow to Obey

God asks us to use our time wisely. He wants us to use our time in a way that honors him. He asked this of the prophet Jonah. God asked him to travel to Nineveh and preach to the people there. Jonah jumped on a ship ... going the other direction! He soon found out that it does not pay to be slow to obey. God stopped him in his tracks, and while Jonah was delayed in a very interesting place, he used the time to pray and decide to obey.

A message from the LORD came to Jonah, the son of Amittai.

The LORD said, "Go to the great city of Nineveh. Preach against it. The sins of its people have come to my attention."

But Jonah ran away from the LORD. He headed for Tarshish. So he went down to the port of Joppa. There he found a ship that was going to Tarshish. He paid the fare and went on board. Then he sailed for Tarshish. He was running away from the LORD.

But the LORD sent a strong wind over the Mediterranean Sea. A wild storm came up. It was so wild that the ship was in danger of breaking apart. All the sailors were afraid. Each one cried out to his own god for help. They threw the ship's contents into the sea. They were trying to make the ship lighter.

But Jonah had gone below deck. There he lay down and fell into a deep sleep.   JONAH 1:1–5

The sailors figured out that Jonah was to blame for the terrible storm. They demanded to know who he was and what he was doing.

He answered, "I'm a Hebrew. I worship the LORD. He is the God of heaven. He made the sea and the dry land."

They found out he was running away from the LORD. That's because he had told them. Then they became terrified. So they asked him, "How could you do a thing like that?"

The sea was getting rougher and rougher. So they asked him, "What should we do to you to make the sea calm down?"

"Pick me up and throw me into the sea," he replied. "Then it will become calm. I know it's my fault that this terrible storm has come on you."

But the men didn't do what he said. Instead, they did their best to row back to land. But they couldn't. The sea got even rougher than before. Then they cried out to the LORD. They prayed, "Please, LORD, don't let us die for taking this man's life. After all, he might not be guilty of doing anything wrong. So don't hold us responsible for killing him. LORD, you always do what you want to." Then they took Jonah and threw him overboard. And the stormy sea became calm. The men saw what had happened. Then they began to have great respect for the LORD. They offered a sacrifice to him. And they made promises to him.

Now the LORD sent a huge fish to swallow Jonah. And Jonah was in the belly of the fish for three days and three nights.

JONAH 1:9–17

Jonah spent those three days and nights in the belly of the fish praying to God, repenting for his disobedience, and promising to declare the message of salvation. Then ...

The LORD gave the fish a command. And it spit Jonah up onto dry land. JONAH 2:10

First Things First

When God tells us to do something, we should do it! And, we should do it right away. Getting our own things done first and then doing what God asks second does not work very well, as we shall see. In the Old Testament, God gave the people of Israel an assignment to rebuild the temple in Jerusalem. When outsiders tried to stop them, they became discouraged and stopped working on the temple and spent their time building their houses and planting their crops instead. But this was backwards. God wanted them to spend their time on the temple first, then he would take care of their needs for food and shelter. When they did not do first things first, all of their hard work was a dismal failure.

Here is what the LORD who rules over all says. "The people of Judah say, 'It's not yet time to rebuild the LORD's temple.'"

So the message from the LORD came to me. The LORD said, "My temple is still destroyed. But you are living in your houses that have beautiful wooden walls."

The LORD who rules over all says, "Think carefully about how you are living. You have planted many seeds. But the crops you have gathered are small. So you eat. But you never have enough. You drink. But you are never full. You put on your clothes. But you are not warm. You earn your pay. But it will not buy everything you need."

He continues, "Think carefully about how you are living. Go up into the mountains. Bring logs down. Use them to rebuild the temple, my house. Then I will enjoy it. And you will honor me," says the LORD. You expected a lot. But you can see what a small amount it turned out to be. I blew away what you brought home. I'll tell you why," announces the LORD who rules over all. "Because my temple is still destroyed. In spite of that, each one of you is busy with your own house. So because of what you have done, the heavens have held back the dew. And the earth has not produced its crops. I ordered the rain not to fall on the fields and mountains. Then the ground did not produce any grain. There were not enough grapes to make fresh wine. The trees did not bear enough olives to make oil. People and cattle suffered. All your hard work failed."

HAGGAI 1:2–11

Young Jesus Had the Right Priorities

Unlike Jonah and the Israelites who stopped rebuilding the temple, Jesus never needed to be reminded that his time belonged to God. Even when he was young, Jesus had his priorities straight.

Every year Jesus' parents went to Jerusalem for the Passover Feast. When Jesus was 12 years old, they went up to the feast as usual. After the feast was over, his parents left to go back home. The boy Jesus stayed behind in Jerusalem. But they were not aware of it. They thought he was somewhere in their group. So they traveled on for a day. Then they began to look for him among their relatives and friends. They did not find him. So they went back to Jerusalem to look for him. After three days they found him in the temple courtyard. He was sitting with the teachers. He was listening to them and asking them questions. Everyone who heard him was amazed at how much he understood. They also were amazed at his answers. When his parents saw him, they were amazed. His mother said to him, "Son, why have you treated us like this? Your father and I have been worried about you. We have been looking for you everywhere."

"Why were you looking for me?" he asked. "Didn't you know I had to be in my Father's house?"   LUKE 2:41–49

Discussion Questions:

1. In our first two stories, God gave assignments to people. What did Jonah do when he got his assignment? What did the people of Judah do? Why do you think they did not do God's assignment first?

2. God delayed Jonah and caused the efforts of the people of Judah to fail in order to get them to obey and put first things first. Have you ever learned a good lesson because of a frustrating delay or a failure?

3. Our key verse, Colossians 3:17, says to "do everything you say or do in the name of the Lord Jesus." Can it really mean "everything?" How?

Giving My Resources

KEY QUESTION:
How do I best use my resources to serve God and others?

KEY IDEA:
I give my resources to help God's plan.

KEY VERSE:
You do well in everything else. You do well in faith and in speaking. You do well in knowledge and in complete commitment. And you do well in the love we have helped to start in you. So make sure that you also do well in the grace of giving to others.   *2 Corinthians 8:7*

THINK ABOUT IT

In the time of the Old Testament, God's people gave God a tenth of everything they had. This is called tithing. People gave God the first (or the best) tenth of their crops, their live-stock or their money. This showed God he was number one in their lives. God still wants us to give him our first and our best. For instance, when we make money, we should first give some of it to God before we spend any of it on ourselves. When we are serving, we should give our best efforts and not be a half-hearted worker. God wants our first and our best.

When We Don't Give Enough

For some of us, the more we have, the harder it is to give it away. Having a lot of money doesn't necessarily mean we are good at sharing what we have. Strangely, if we hoard our money for ourselves instead of giving the first part to God, we may never feel like we have enough. King Solomon was a very rich man. In the book of Ecclesiastes, he wrote about the dangers of wealth. Money itself is not evil, but the love of money leads to sin. More wealth does not mean more happiness.

> Anyone who loves money never has enough.
>> Anyone who loves wealth is never satisfied with what
>>> they get.
>> That doesn't have any meaning either.
>
> As more and more goods are made,
>> more and more people use them up.
> So how can those goods benefit their owners?
>> All they can do is look at them with desire.
>
> The sleep of a worker is sweet.
>> It doesn't matter whether they eat a little or a lot.
> But the wealth of rich people
>> keeps them awake at night.　　Ecclesiastes 5:10–12

People who love their wealth too much are forgetting one thing: they can't take any of it with them when they die. Money doesn't do anyone any good after this life, so we might as well do good with it while we are here.

> Everyone is born naked.
>> They come into the world with nothing.
>> And they go out of it with nothing.
> They don't get anything from their work
>> that they can take with them.   ECCLESIASTES 5:15

Curiously, some of the richest people in the world are some of the unhappiest. They might be missing the fact that everything they have is a gift from God. Even the ability to enjoy what they have is a gift from God.

Sometimes God gives a person wealth and possessions. God makes it possible for that person to enjoy them. God helps them accept the life he has given them. God helps them to be happy in their work. All these things are gifts from God.   ECCLESIASTES 5:19

The Joy of Giving

When the Israelites were living in the wilderness, God asked Moses to build a tabernacle, or holy tent, for him. Moses gave the people a long list of the building materials and craftsmen they would need to accomplish this big project. Even though the people were living in tough conditions, they gave of their time and treasures willingly. They gave so much that Moses had to tell them to stop!

Everyone who wanted to give offerings to the LORD brought them to him. The offerings were for the work on the tent of meeting. They were also for the sacred clothes and for any other purpose at the tent. Every man and woman who wanted to give came. They brought gold jewelry of all kinds. They brought pins, earrings, rings and other jewelry. All of them gave their gold as a wave offering to the LORD. People brought what they had. They brought blue, purple or bright red yarn or fine linen. They brought goat hair, ram skins dyed red, or the other kind of strong leather. Some brought silver or bronze as an offering to the LORD. Others brought acacia wood for any part of the work. All the skilled women spun yarn with their hands. They brought blue, purple or bright red yarn or fine linen. All the skilled women who wanted to spin the goat hair did so. The leaders brought onyx stones and other jewels for the linen apron and the chest cloth. They also brought spices and olive oil. They brought them for the light, for the anointing oil, and for the sweet-smelling incense. All the men and women of Israel who wanted to bring offerings to the LORD brought them to him. The offerings were for all the work the LORD had commanded Moses to tell them to do.

EXODUS 35:21–29

They received from Moses all the offerings the people of Israel had brought. They had brought the offerings for all the work for every purpose connected with the holy tent. That included setting it up. The people kept bringing the offerings they chose to give. They brought them morning after morning. So all the skilled workers working on the holy tent stopped what they were doing. They said to Moses, "The LORD commanded us to do the work. And the people are bringing more than enough for us to do it."

Then Moses gave an order. A message was sent through the whole camp. It said, "No man or woman should make anything else and offer it for the holy tent." And so the people were kept from bringing more offerings.   EXODUS 36:3–6

Giving Our Best

Sometime after Jesus was born, wise men arrived who had come to worship him. For these men, worshiping Jesus meant giving him their best, which was more than we might think. They gave him months of their time as they traveled from a far-away land to see him. They were honored men, yet they humbled themselves and bowed their knees to give their worship to Jesus. And they gave him valuable treasures from their land, costly gifts that were the best they had to give.

Jesus was born in Bethlehem in Judea. This happened while Herod was king of Judea. After Jesus' birth, Wise Men from the

east came to Jerusalem. They asked, "Where is the child who has been born to be king of the Jews? We saw his star when it rose. Now we have come to worship him."

When King Herod heard about it, he was very upset. Everyone in Jerusalem was troubled too. So Herod called together all the chief priests of the people. He also called the teachers of the law. He asked them where the Messiah was going to be born. "In Bethlehem in Judea," they replied.   MATTHEW 2:1–5A

Then Herod secretly called for the Wise Men. He found out from them exactly when the star had appeared. He sent them to Bethlehem. He said, "Go and search carefully for the child. As soon as you find him, report it to me. Then I can go and worship him too."

After the Wise Men had listened to the king, they went on their way. The star they had seen when it rose went ahead of them. It finally stopped over the place where the child was. When they saw the star, they were filled with joy. The Wise Men went to the house. There they saw the child with his mother Mary. They bowed down and worshiped him. Then they opened their treasures. They gave him gold, frankincense and myrrh. But God warned them in a dream not to go back to Herod. So they returned to their country on a different road.   MATTHEW 2:7–12

Discussion Questions:

1. In our key verse, 2 Corinthians 8:7, what things did the people of Corinth already do well, and what were they to make sure they did well? Based on what we learned about giving our first and our best, what advice would you give someone who wanted to be a better giver?

2. What are some differences between the rich person that Solomon talked about in Ecclesiastes and the wise men who visited Jesus?

3. Why do you think the Israelites gave so much they had to be asked to stop? Have you ever felt that much joy when you gave? In what ways does giving give back to the giver?

Sharing My Faith

🔑 **KEY QUESTION:**
How do I share my faith with those who don't know God?

🔑 **KEY IDEA:**
I share my faith with others to help God's plan.

🔑 **KEY VERSE:**
Pray also for me. Pray that whenever I speak, the right words will be given to me. Then I can be bold as I tell the mystery of the good news. Because of the good news, I am being held by chains as the Lord's messenger. So pray that I will be bold as I preach the good news. That's what I should do. *Ephesians 6:19–20*

THINK ABOUT IT

One of the most important things we can give to others is our faith. Sharing our faith is something every child of God is called to do. Reading this book can help us get better at explaining what we believe.

Sharing Our Faith Is Never Wasted

Sometimes when you share your faith, people will reject it. This doesn't mean that you shouldn't have shared. Even if it doesn't feel like you are making a difference, you are. Remember Jonah? He avoided God's command to go to Nineveh, because he thought the people in Nineveh were beyond saving. When we read the first part of his story (chapter 18), we left him when he had just been spit up on a beach by the big fish. Now we get to read the rest of the story. See what happened when he finally obeyed God, even when he didn't think the people would respond.

Jonah obeyed the LORD. He went to Nineveh. It was a very large city. In fact, it took about three days to go through it. Jonah began by going one whole day into the city. As he went, he announced, "In 40 days Nineveh will be destroyed." The people of Nineveh believed God's warning.   JONAH 3:3–5A

Jonah's warning reached the king of Nineveh. He got up from his throne. He took off his royal robes. He also dressed himself in the clothing of sadness. And then he sat down in the dust. Here is the message he sent out to the people of Nineveh.   JONAH 3:6–7A

"Let people and animals alike be covered with the clothing of sadness. All of you must call out to God with all your hearts. Stop doing what is evil. Don't harm others. Who knows? God might take pity on us. He might not be angry with us anymore. Then we won't die."

God saw what they did. He saw that they stopped doing what was evil. So he took pity on them. He didn't destroy them as he had said he would.   JONAH 3:8–10

It's Not What You Say, It's How You Say It

We can all learn a lesson from watching how Jesus talked to people. The woman in Samaria was not used to having people speak kindly to her or care about her. So when Jesus met her at the well, the manner in which he spoke to her said more to her than his words.

A woman from Samaria came to get some water. Jesus said to her, "Will you give me a drink?" His disciples had gone into the town to buy food.

The Samaritan woman said to him, "You are a Jew. I am a Samaritan woman. How can you ask me for a drink?" She said this because Jews don't have anything to do with Samaritans.

Jesus answered her, "You do not know what God's gift is. And

you do not know who is asking you for a drink. If you did, you would have asked him. He would have given you living water."

"Sir," the woman said, "you don't have anything to get water with. The well is deep. Where can you get this living water? Our father Jacob gave us the well. He drank from it himself. So did his sons and his livestock. Are you more important than he is?"

Jesus answered, "Everyone who drinks this water will be thirsty again. But anyone who drinks the water I give them will never be thirsty. In fact, the water I give them will become a spring of water in them. It will flow up into eternal life."

The woman said to him, "Sir, give me this water. Then I will never be thirsty. And I won't have to keep coming here to get water."

He told her, "Go. Get your husband and come back."

"I have no husband," she replied.

Jesus said to her, "You are right when you say you have no husband. The fact is, you have had five husbands. And the man you live with now is not your husband. What you have just said is very true."   JOHN 4:7–18

The woman must have been shocked that Jesus knew so much about her. She brought up the difference between the religious practices of the Samaritans and those of the Jews. But Jesus told her the way people worship is not as important as who they worship. Then he trusted her with some very important news: he told her he was the Messiah.

The woman left her water jar and went back to the town. She said to the people, "Come. See a man who told me everything I've ever done. Could this be the Messiah?"   JOHN 4:28–29

Many of the Samaritans from the town of Sychar believed in Jesus. They believed because of what the woman had said about him. She said, "He told me everything I've ever done." Then the Samaritans came to him and tried to get him to stay with them. So he stayed two days. Because of what he said, many more people became believers.

They said to the woman, "We no longer believe just because of what you said. We have now heard for ourselves. We know that this man really is the Savior of the world." JOHN 4:39–42

We Have a Helper

Sharing our faith might seem scary or awkward. We could be afraid we won't know what to say. But in the New Testament God promised us the Holy Spirit as our helper. He gives us the words to say when we need them, just as Paul prays for in our key verse, Ephesians 6:19–20. As we see with Philip, the Holy Spirit even makes sure we meet people at just the right time when they are ready to hear the Good News.

An angel of the Lord spoke to Philip. "Go south to the desert road," he said. "It's the road that goes down from Jerusalem to Gaza." So Philip started out. On his way he met an Ethiopian official. The man had an important position in charge of all the wealth of the Kandake. Kandake means queen of Ethiopia. This official had gone to Jerusalem to worship. On his way home he was sitting in his chariot. He was reading the Book of Isaiah the prophet. The Holy Spirit told Philip, "Go to that chariot. Stay near it."

So Philip ran up to the chariot. He heard the man reading Isaiah the prophet. "Do you understand what you're reading?" Philip asked.

"How can I?" he said. "I need someone to explain it to me." So he invited Philip to come up and sit with him.

Here is the part of Scripture the official was reading. It says,

> "He was led like a sheep to be killed.
>   Just as lambs are silent while their wool is being cut off,
>   he did not open his mouth."   ACTS 8:26–32

The official said to Philip, "Tell me, please. Who is the prophet talking about? Himself, or someone else?" Then Philip began with that same part of Scripture. He told him the good news about Jesus.

As they traveled along the road, they came to some water. The official said, "Look! Here is water! What can stop me from being baptized?" He gave orders to stop the chariot. Then both Philip and the official went down into the water. Philip baptized him.

ACTS 8:34–38

Discussion Questions:

1. Do you know someone who is not interested in hearing about Jesus? In what way could you pray for that person, or for yourself, so that you might be able to talk with him or her about your faith?

2. It was an unlikely person who invited her whole town to meet Jesus and believe in him. In what ways did Jesus treat the woman at the well that caused her to respond so positively to him?

3. Have you ever "run into" someone that could have been a person God wanted you to share your faith with? Who? Say our key verse out loud as your own prayer to help you be ready the next time that happens.

Who Am I Becoming?

I am the vine. You are the branches.
If you remain joined to me, and I to you,
you will bear a lot of fruit.
You can't do anything without me.
John 15:5

As we learn to *think* and *act* like Jesus, we begin to *become* (or look) more like him. But becoming like Jesus does not happen quickly. It's a slow process.

In the verse above, Jesus compares living the Christian life to a vine bearing lots of fruit. Jesus is the vine, and we are the branches. A grapevine produces delicious, juicy grapes, but this happens over time. And if you cut off one of the branches, would you keep getting leaves and buds and flowers and then grapes on it? Of course not. In order for the grapes to grow and ripen, the branch must remain connected to the vine to receive water and nutrients. In the same way, we must stay connected to Jesus so we can bear good fruit.

These final ten chapters talk about ten key virtues (or fruit) that God wants to grow in your life. Are you connected to him? Can you say, "I am growing this fruit in my life"?

1. Love
2. Joy
3. Peace
4. Self-Control
5. Hope

6. Patience
7. Kindness/Goodness
8. Faithfulness
9. Gentleness
10. Humility

I can do all this by the power of Christ.
He gives me strength.
Philippians 4:13

21

Love

⚲ KEY QUESTION:

What does it mean to sacrificially, unconditionally love others?

⚲ KEY IDEA:

I will try hard to love God and love others.

⚲ KEY VERSE:

Here is what love is. It is not that we loved God. It is that he loved us and sent his Son to give his life to pay for our sins. Dear friends, since God loved us this much, we should also love one another. No one has ever seen God. But if we love one another, God lives in us. His love is made complete in us.   *1 John 4:10–12*

THINK ABOUT IT

We are starting our last ten beliefs, the beliefs that help us to "be" like Jesus. When we live out these beliefs, people will see character qualities of Jesus in our lives. The quality Jesus said was most important is love. When we love others, according to our key verse we are showing them what God looks like.

A Loving Example: David and Jonathan

The Old Testament offers us a great example of a loving friendship in David and Jonathan. Jonathan was the son of King Saul, so everyone assumed he would be Israel's next king. But when young David came on the scene, it was clear God had other plans. We might expect that Jonathan would become jealous of David and even hate him. But just the opposite happened. The two became best friends. But Saul became jealous of David and wanted to kill him.

Jonathan and David became close friends. Jonathan loved David just as he loved himself. From that time on, Saul kept David with him. He didn't let him return home to his family. Jonathan made a covenant with David because he loved him just as he loved himself. Jonathan took off the robe he was wearing and gave it to David. He also gave him his military clothes. He even gave him his sword, his bow and his belt.   1 SAMUEL 18:1B–4

Saul told his son Jonathan and all the attendants to kill David. But Jonathan liked David very much. So Jonathan warned him, "My father Saul is looking for a chance to kill you. Be very careful tomorrow morning. Find a place to hide and stay there. My father and I will come and stand in the field where you are hiding. I'll speak to him about you. Then I'll tell you what I find out."

Jonathan told his father Saul some good things about David. He said to him, "Please don't do anything to harm David. He hasn't done anything to harm you. And what he's done has helped you a lot. He put his own life in danger when he killed Goliath. The LORD used him to win a great battle for the whole nation of Israel. When you saw it, you were glad. So why would you do anything to harm a man like David? He isn't guilty of doing anything to harm you. Why would you want to kill him without any reason?"

Saul paid attention to Jonathan. Saul made a promise. He said, "You can be sure that the LORD lives. And you can be just as sure that David will not be put to death."   1 SAMUEL 19:1–6

Jonathan saved David's life, but the peace didn't last long. Saul became jealous of David again and wanted to kill him. David ran away from Saul and stayed in hiding. Eventually he found his way back to Jonathan. The two friends came up with a plan to make sure David stayed safe.

Jonathan said to David, "Tomorrow is the time for the New Moon feast. You will be missed, because your seat at the table will be empty. Go to the place where you hid when all this trouble began. Go there the day after tomorrow, when evening is approaching. There's a stone out there called Ezel. Wait by it. I'll shoot three arrows to one side of the stone. I'll pretend I'm practicing my shooting. Then I'll send a boy out there. I'll tell him, 'Go and find the arrows.' Suppose I say to him, 'The arrows are on this side of you. Bring them here.' Then come. That will mean you are safe. You won't be in any danger. And that's just as sure as the LORD is alive. But suppose I tell the boy, 'The arrows are far beyond you.' Then go. That will mean the LORD is sending you away. And remember what we talked about. Remember that the LORD is a witness between you and me forever."   1 SAMUEL 20:18–23

David and Jonathan carried out their plan. David hid and did not go to dinner. When King Saul asked where David was, Jonathan told his father he had let David do something else instead of coming to eat at the table.

Saul became very angry with Jonathan. He said to him, "You are an evil son. You have refused to obey me. I know that you are on the side of Jesse's son. You should be ashamed of that. And your mother should be ashamed of having a son like you. You will never be king as long as Jesse's son lives on this earth. And you will never have a kingdom either. So send someone to bring the son of Jesse to me. He must die!"

"Why do you want to put him to death?" Jonathan asked his father. "What has he done?" But Saul threw his spear at Jonathan to kill him. Then Jonathan knew that his father wanted to kill David.

So Jonathan got up from the table. He was very angry. On that second day of the feast, he refused to eat. He was very sad that his father was treating David so badly.

The next morning Jonathan went out to the field to meet David. He took a young boy with him. He said to the boy, "Run and find the arrows I shoot." As the boy ran, Jonathan shot an arrow far beyond him. The boy came to the place where Jonathan's arrow had fallen. Then Jonathan shouted to him, "The arrow went far beyond you, didn't it?" He continued, "Hurry up! Run fast! Don't stop!" The boy picked up the arrow and returned to his

master. The boy didn't know what was going on. Only Jonathan and David knew. Jonathan gave his weapons to the boy. He told him, "Go back to town. Take the weapons with you."

After the boy had gone, David got up from the south side of the stone. He bowed down in front of Jonathan with his face to the ground. He did it three times. Then they kissed each other and cried. But David cried more than Jonathan did.

Jonathan said to David, "Go in peace. In the name of the LORD we've promised to be friends. We have said, 'The LORD is a witness between you and me. He's a witness between your children and my children forever.'" Then David left, and Jonathan went back to the town.   1 SAMUEL 20:30–42

The Good Shepherd Gives His Life for His Sheep

Jonathan had to send David away for his own protection, and David hid from Saul for several years before he eventually became king. Jonathan risked his life for David. He was willing to die for him. Does that remind you of someone? That's how much Jesus loves you—enough to die for you. Jesus said:

"I am the good shepherd. The good shepherd gives his life for the sheep. The hired man is not the shepherd and does not own the sheep. So when the hired man sees the wolf coming, he leaves the sheep and runs away. Then the wolf attacks the flock and scatters it. The man runs away because he is a hired man. He does not care about the sheep.

"I am the good shepherd. I know my sheep, and my sheep know me. They know me just as the Father knows me and I know the Father. And I give my life for the sheep. I have other sheep that do not belong to this sheep pen. I must bring them in too. They also will listen to my voice. Then there will be one flock and one shepherd. The reason my Father loves me is that I give up my life. But I will take it back again. No one takes it from me. I give it up myself. I have the authority to give it up. And I have the authority to take it back again. I received this command from my Father."   JOHN 10:11–18

Discussion Questions:

1. Who is one of your best friends? What makes this friendship so special?

2. In what ways did Jonathan show love to David? How can you show love to people who are being treated unfairly?

3. Our key verse, 1 John 4:10–12, tells us how it is possible to love one another. How does love get started in us? Why does it help us to love better when we know how much God loved us first?

Joy

🔑 **KEY QUESTION:**
What gives us true happiness and contentment in life?

🔑 **KEY IDEA:**
No matter what happens, I feel happy inside and understand God's plan for my life.

🔑 **KEY VERSE:**
I have told you this so that you will have the same joy that I have. I also want your joy to be complete. *John 15:11*

THINK ABOUT IT

Our key verse contains words spoken by Jesus. Jesus wants us to have the same joy as he has. He wants our joy to be complete. But aren't there times when we don't have complete joy? We received joy when Jesus came to the world, we celebrate with joy when we hear God's Word, and yes, we can have joy even when things in our lives are difficult.

Joy Came When Jesus Came

Have you ever noticed how often people use the word "joy" around Christmas time? Jesus' coming to earth was the most joyous occasion in our world's history. The New Testament begins with the arrival of our Savior, and everyone who saw him certainly had reason to have joy! This is the same joy Jesus brings with him when he arrives in our lives.

While Joseph and Mary were [in Bethlehem], the time came for the child to be born. She gave birth to her first baby. It was a boy. She wrapped him in large strips of cloth. Then she placed him in a manger. That's because there was no guest room where they could stay.

There were shepherds living out in the fields nearby. It was night, and they were taking care of their sheep. An angel of the Lord appeared to them. And the glory of the Lord shone around them. They were terrified. But the angel said to them, "Do not be afraid. I bring you good news. It will bring great joy for all the people. Today in the town of David a Savior has been born to you. He is the Messiah, the Lord. Here is how you will know I am telling you the truth. You will find a baby wrapped in strips of cloth and lying in a manger."

Suddenly a large group of angels from heaven also appeared. They were praising God. They said,

> "May glory be given to God in the highest heaven!
> And may peace be given to those he is pleased with
> on earth!"

The angels left and went into heaven. Then the shepherds said to one another, "Let's go to Bethlehem. Let's see this thing that has happened, which the Lord has told us about."

So they hurried off and found Mary and Joseph and the baby. The baby was lying in the manger. After the shepherds had seen him, they told everyone. They reported what the angel had said about this child. All who heard it were amazed at what the shepherds said to them. But Mary kept all these things like a secret treasure in her heart. She thought about them over and over. The shepherds returned. They gave glory and praise to God. Everything they had seen and heard was just as they had been told.

LUKE 2:6–20

Joy Is Found in the Word of God

Sometimes we lose our joy because our own mistakes make us sad. We may feel bad about our sin, especially when we hear what the Word of God has to say about it. This may not feel much like joy at the moment, but we can have joy because we can be forgiven. We can take joy in God's mercy.

In the book of Nehemiah in the Old Testament, the Israelites felt badly (they were convicted) when they heard God's

Word (the Law) for the first time in a long time. They began to cry, but Nehemiah told them to stop. He told them to celebrate because they had been able to hear and understand the Word of the Lord.

Ezra the priest brought the Law out to the whole community. It was the first day of the seventh month. The group was made up of men, women, and children old enough to understand what Ezra was going to read. He read the Law to them from sunrise until noon. He did it as he faced the open area in front of the Water Gate. He read it to the men, the women, and the children old enough to understand. And all the people paid careful attention as Ezra was reading the Book of the Law.   NEHEMIAH 8:2–3

Nehemiah was the governor. Ezra was a priest and the teacher of the Law. They spoke up. So did the Levites who were teaching the people. All these men said to the people, "This day is set apart to honor the LORD your God. So don't weep. Don't be sad." All the people had been weeping as they listened to the words of the Law.

Nehemiah said, "Go and enjoy some good food and sweet drinks. Send some of it to people who don't have any. This day is holy to our Lord. So don't be sad. The joy of the LORD makes you strong."

The Levites calmed all the people down. They said, "Be quiet. This is a holy day. So don't be sad."

Then all the people went away to eat and drink. They shared their food with others. They celebrated with great joy. Now they understood the words they had heard. That's because everything had been explained to them.   NEHEMIAH 8:9–12

So the people went out and brought back some branches. They built themselves booths on their own roofs. They made them in their courtyards. They put them up in the courtyards of the house of God. They built them in the open area in front of the Water Gate. And they built them in the open area in front of the Gate of Ephraim. All the people who had returned from the land of Babylon made booths. They lived in them during the Feast of Booths. They hadn't celebrated the feast with so much joy for a long time. In fact, they had never celebrated it like that from the days of Joshua, the son of Nun, until that day. So their joy was very great.   NEHEMIAH 8:16–17

Joy Is Ours No Matter What

Hearing God's Word and doing what it says doesn't necessarily lead to an easy life. In fact, the opposite might be true. Following Jesus may make life harder. As you read the rest of this chapter, look for all the ways our lives can be difficult. It might seem strange, but the hard things in life can lead to joy. Because we find new strength, we learn to be content, and our faith is proven real.

My brothers and sisters, you will face all kinds of trouble. When you do, think of it as pure joy. Your faith will be tested. You know that when this happens it will produce in you the strength to continue. And you must allow this strength to finish its work. Then you will be all you should be. You will have everything you need. If any of you needs wisdom, you should ask God for it. He will give it to you. God gives freely to everyone and doesn't find fault.   JAMES 1:2–5

I have learned to be content no matter what happens to me. I know what it's like not to have what I need. I also know what it's like to have more than I need. I have learned the secret of being content no matter what happens. I am content whether I am well fed or hungry. I am content whether I have more than enough or not enough. I can do all this by the power of Christ. He gives me strength.   PHILIPPIANS 4:11B–13

Because you know all this, you have great joy. You have joy even though you may have had to suffer for a little while. You may have had to suffer sadness in all kinds of trouble. Your troubles have come in order to prove that your faith is real. Your faith is worth more than gold. That's because gold can pass away even when fire has made it pure. Your faith is meant to bring praise, honor and glory to God. This will happen when Jesus Christ returns. Even though you have not seen him, you love him. Though you do not see him now, you believe in him. You are filled with a glorious joy that can't be put into words. You are receiving the salvation of your souls. This salvation is the final result of your faith.   1 PETER 1:6–9

Discussion Questions:

1. How do you describe true joy? Is it a feeling?

2. One key to joy is being content — choosing to be satisfied with what we have, no matter how much or how little it is. Why do you suppose Philippians 4:11–13 says we have to learn to be content when we have more than enough? Have you experienced having more than enough, yet not being content or joyful?

3. If Jesus said in our key verse, John 15:11, that he wants our joy to be complete, how does he make that happen? How can our joy be complete when we are having a bad day?

23

Peace

O—π KEY QUESTION:

Where do I find strength to battle worry and fear?

O—π KEY IDEA:

I am not worried because I have found peace with God, peace with others and peace with myself.

O—π KEY VERSE:

Don't worry about anything. No matter what happens, tell God about everything. Ask and pray, and give thanks to him. Then God's peace will watch over your hearts and your minds. He will do this because you belong to Christ Jesus. God's peace can never be completely understood.

Philippians 4:6–7

THINK ABOUT IT

In the previous chapter, we learned we can have joy even when we have problems. In this chapter, our key verse says we can have peace even when we have something to worry about! God's peace is ours when we pray about everything and obey him. If we are not at peace with a friend or relative, putting the other person first is a great way to solve the problem. And even when we are the most stressed, knowing Jesus is in control gives us peace.

Peace with Others

One of the biggest ways our peace gets disturbed is when we are not getting along with somebody. Even just one small disagreement can make us feel upset. We need to have peace with others in order to feel peace inside.

In the Old Testament, Abram (later called Abraham) and his nephew Lot moved from place to place together. When those who took care of their animal herds began to disagree over land, it caused a problem between Abram and Lot. Abram quickly settled the argument by giving Lot his choice of land to settle on. Abram showed how important it is to put others' needs ahead of our own in order to make peace.

Lot was moving around with Abram. Lot also had flocks and herds and tents. But the land didn't have enough food for both Abram and Lot. They had large herds and many servants, so they weren't able to stay together. The people who took care of Abram's herds and those who took care of Lot's herds began to argue. The Canaanites and Perizzites were also living in the land at that time.

So Abram said to Lot, "Let's not argue with each other. The people taking care of your herds and those taking care of mine shouldn't argue with one another either. After all, we're part of the same family. Isn't the whole land in front of you? Let's separate. If you go to the left, I'll go to the right. If you go to the right, I'll go to the left."   GENESIS 13:5–9

Lot looked around and chose the land that looked better. Abram let Lot have the first pick, even though that left him with land that looked barren. Yet God rewarded Abram for trusting God and keeping peace with his nephew. When we put others first, we ourselves are blessed.

The LORD spoke to Abram after Lot had left him. He said, "Look around from where you are. Look north and south, east and west. I will give you all the land you see. I will give it forever to you and your family who comes after you. I will make them like the dust of the earth. Can dust be counted? If it can, then your family can be counted. Go! Walk through the land. See how long and wide it is. I am giving it to you."

So Abram went to live near the large trees of Mamre at

Hebron. There he pitched his tents and built an altar to honor the LORD.   GENESIS 13:14–18

Peace with God

The secret to keeping peace with God is obedience to God. When King Solomon was a young man, he had a wonderful relationship with God, and he asked God for something that pleased God very much. But look carefully for one way Solomon was not obeying God at first: He was offering sacrifices in the high places where idol worship took place. Yet, after his dream, he went to the proper place to offer sacrifices to God. God rewarded Solomon's obedience by keeping his kingdom at peace.

Solomon showed his love for the LORD. He did it by obeying the laws his father David had taught him. But Solomon offered sacrifices at the high places. He also burned incense there.

King Solomon went to the city of Gibeon to offer sacrifices. That's where the most important high place was. There he offered 1,000 burnt offerings on the altar. The LORD appeared to Solomon at Gibeon. He spoke to him in a dream during the night. God said, "Ask for anything you want me to give you."

Solomon answered, "You have been very kind to my father David, your servant. That's because he was faithful to you. He did what was right. His heart was honest. And you have continued to be very kind to him. You have given him a son to sit on his throne this day.

"LORD my God, you have now made me king. You have put me in the place of my father David. But I'm only a little child. I don't know how to carry out my duties. I'm here among the people you have chosen. They are a great nation. They are more than anyone can count. So give me a heart that understands. Then I can rule over your people. I can tell the difference between what is right and what is wrong. Who can possibly rule over this great nation of yours?"

The Lord was pleased that Solomon had asked for that. So God said to him, "You have not asked to live for a long time. You have not asked to be wealthy. You have not even asked to have your enemies killed. Instead, you have asked for wisdom. You want to do what is right and fair when you judge people. Because that is what you have asked for, I will give it to you. I will give you a wise and understanding heart. So here is what will be true of you. There has never been anyone like you. And there never will be. And that is not all. I will give you what you have not asked for. I will give you wealth and honor. As long as you live, no other king will be as great as you are. Live the way I want you to. Obey my laws and commands, just as your father David did. Then I will let you live for a long time." Solomon woke up. He realized he had been dreaming.

He returned to Jerusalem. He stood in front of the ark of the Lord's covenant. He sacrificed burnt offerings and friendship offerings. Then he gave a feast for all his officials.   1 KINGS 3:3–15

Solomon ruled over all the kingdoms that were west of the Euphrates River. He ruled from Tiphsah all the way to Gaza. And he had peace and rest on every side. While Solomon was king, Judah

and Israel lived in safety. They were secure from Dan all the way to Beersheba. Everyone had their own vine and their own fig tree.

1 KINGS 4:24–25

Peace with Yourself

A relationship with Jesus allows us to have peace in our hearts. No matter what is going on, no matter what seems to be going wrong, we know that God will take care of us. When trouble comes, and it will, we need to remember that Jesus is still in control. One night, Jesus proved this to his disciples in an amazing way!

When evening came, Jesus said to his disciples, "Let's go over to the other side of the lake." They left the crowd behind. And they took him along in a boat, just as he was. There were also other boats with him. A wild storm came up. Waves crashed over the boat. It was about to sink. Jesus was in the back, sleeping on a cushion. The disciples woke him up. They said, "Teacher! Don't you care if we drown?"

He got up and ordered the wind to stop. He said to the waves, "Quiet! Be still!" Then the wind died down. And it was completely calm.

He said to his disciples, "Why are you so afraid? Don't you have any faith at all yet?"

They were terrified. They asked each other, "Who is this? Even the wind and the waves obey him!"   MARK 4:35–41

Discussion Questions:

1. We saw in the life of Abram how letting others go first can help us have peace with other people. When is it hard for you to let others go first?

2. When have you seen Jesus calm a "storm" (a stressful situation) in your life?

3. What does our key verse, Philippians 4:6–7, say we should do in order to have God's peace? Do you think it's possible to feel peaceful even when there is something you are worried about?

24

Self-Control

KEY QUESTION:

How does God free me from sin and bad habits?

KEY IDEA:

I have the power through Jesus to control myself.

KEY VERSE:

God's grace has now appeared. By his grace, God offers to save all people. His grace teaches us to say no to godless ways and sinful desires. We must control ourselves. We must do what is right. We must lead godly lives in today's world. That's how we should live as we wait for the blessed hope God has given us. We are waiting for Jesus Christ to appear in his glory. He is our great God and Savior.

Titus 2:11–13

THINK ABOUT IT

Self-control can be one of the most difficult areas to master. The pull of our desires is strong, and we like to give ourselves whatever we want. Yet what we want can lead to something we don't want. Samson did not have self-control, and he lost his strength. The prodigal son did not have self-control, and he thought he lost his place in the family. Resisting our own desires is something we can only do with God's power from the Holy Spirit. If we fail, it's wonderful to know God is ready to give us a second chance through his grace and forgiveness.

Strong yet Weak

Samson was a special leader in the Old Testament who was born under Nazirite vows, which included a vow not to cut his hair. God blessed Samson with supernatural strength. Samson knew that in order to keep this strength, he had to keep his promise not to cut his hair. But he did not have the internal strength—the self-control—he needed to keep his vow. Because he had weak self-control, he became a physical weakling, and his enemies put him under their control in prison.

Samson fell in love again. The woman lived in the Valley of Sorek. Her name was Delilah. The rulers of the Philistines went to her. They said, "See if you can get him to tell you the secret of why he's so strong. Find out how we can overpower him. Then we can tie him up. We can bring him under our control. Each of us will give you 28 pounds of silver."

So Delilah said to Samson, "Tell me the secret of why you are so strong. Tell me how you can be tied up and controlled."

Samson answered her, "Let someone tie me up with seven new bowstrings. They must be strings that aren't completely dry. Then I'll become as weak as any other man."

So the Philistine rulers brought seven new bowstrings to her. They weren't completely dry. Delilah tied Samson up with them. Men were hiding in the room. She called out to him, "Samson! The Philistines are attacking you!" But he snapped the bowstrings easily. They were like pieces of string that had come too close to a flame. So the secret of why he was so strong wasn't discovered.

Delilah spoke to Samson again. "You have made me look foolish," she said. "You told me a lie. Come on. Tell me how you can be tied up."

Samson said, "Let someone tie me tightly with new ropes. They must be ropes that have never been used. Then I'll become as weak as any other man."

So Delilah got some new ropes. She tied him up with them. Men were hiding in the room. She called out to him, "Samson! The Philistines are attacking you!" But he snapped the ropes off his arms. They fell off just as if they were threads.

Delilah spoke to Samson again. "All this time you have been

making me look foolish," she said. "You have been telling me lies. This time really tell me how you can be tied up."

He replied, "Weave the seven braids of my hair into the cloth on a loom. Then tighten the cloth with a pin. If you do, I'll become as weak as any other man." So while Samson was sleeping, Delilah took hold of the seven braids of his hair. She wove them into the cloth on a loom. Then she tightened the cloth with a pin.

Again she called out to him, "Samson! The Philistines are attacking you!" He woke up from his sleep. He pulled up the pin and the loom, together with the cloth.

Then she said to him, "How can you say, 'I love you'? You won't even share your secret with me. This is the third time you have made me look foolish. And you still haven't told me the secret of why you are so strong." She continued to pester him day after day. She nagged him until he was sick and tired of it.

So he told her everything. He said, "My hair has never been cut. That's because I've been a Nazirite since the day I was born. A Nazirite is set apart to God. If you shave my head, I won't be strong anymore. I'll become as weak as any other man."

Delilah realized he had told her everything. So she sent a message to the Philistine rulers. She said, "Come back one more time. He has told me everything." So the rulers returned. They brought the silver with them. Delilah got Samson to go to sleep on her lap. Then she called for someone to shave off the seven braids of his hair. That's how she began to bring Samson under her control. And he wasn't strong anymore.

She called out, "Samson! The Philistines are attacking you!"

He woke up from his sleep. He thought, "I'll go out just as I did before. I'll shake myself free." But he didn't know that the LORD had left him.

Then the Philistines grabbed him. They poked his eyes out. They took him down to Gaza. They put bronze chains around him. Then they made him grind grain in the prison. Judges 16:4–21

When the Philistines gathered for a celebration to their gods, they brought Samson out to make fun of him. But Samson asked the servant to put him near the pillars that held up the

temple. Then he prayed for God to return his strength and pun-
ish the Philistines.

Then he prayed to the LORD. Samson said, "LORD and King,
show me that you still have concern for me. Please, God, make
me strong just one more time. Let me pay the Philistines back for
what they did to my two eyes. Let me do it with only one blow."
Then Samson reached toward the two pillars that were in the
middle of the temple. They were the ones that held up the temple.
He put his right hand on one of them. He put his left hand on
the other. He leaned hard against them. Samson said, "Let me die
together with the Philistines!" Then he pushed with all his might.
The temple came down on the rulers. It fell on all the people in
it. So Samson killed many more Philistines when he died than he
did while he lived.   JUDGES 16:28–30

Where Lack of Self-Control Leads

*Samson tried very hard to keep his vow, but he did not have the
willpower to resist Delilah's pressure. In the New Testament,
Jesus told a story about a young man who did not even try to
live right. He gave himself every kind of pleasure until he grew
sick of his life and was embarrassed to return to his father. Like
the young man's father, our heavenly Father knows we struggle.
He sent his only Son to make up the difference in the gap of
self-control in our lives. He wants for us to come home to him
no matter our condition.*

Jesus continued, "There was a man who had two sons. The
younger son spoke to his father. He said, 'Father, give me my
share of the family property.' So the father divided his property
between his two sons.

"Not long after that, the younger son packed up all he had.
Then he left for a country far away. There he wasted his money
on wild living. He spent everything he had. Then the whole country ran low on food. So the son didn't have what he needed. He
went to work for someone who lived in that country. That person
sent the son to the fields to feed the pigs. The son wanted to fill

his stomach with the food the pigs were eating. But no one gave him anything.

"Then he began to think clearly again. He said, 'How many of my father's hired servants have more than enough food! But here I am dying from hunger! I will get up and go back to my father. I will say to him, "Father, I have sinned against heaven. And I have sinned against you. I am no longer fit to be called your son. Make me like one of your hired servants."' So he got up and went to his father.

"While the son was still a long way off, his father saw him. He was filled with tender love for his son. He ran to him. He threw his arms around him and kissed him.

"The son said to him, 'Father, I have sinned against heaven and against you. I am no longer fit to be called your son.'

"But the father said to his servants, 'Quick! Bring the best robe and put it on him. Put a ring on his finger and sandals on his feet. Bring the fattest calf and kill it. Let's have a feast and celebrate. This son of mine was dead. And now he is alive again. He was lost. And now he is found.' So they began to celebrate.   LUKE 15:11–24

Discussion Questions:

1. In what areas do you struggle the most with self-control?

2. Are you more like Samson who gave in to pressure from others, or more like the young man, who ran after every kind of fun and pleasure?

3. Our key verse, Titus 2:11–13, says God "teaches us to say no to godless ways and sinful desires." Why would we want to try to say no if it is so hard to resist what we want to do?

Hope

🗝 KEY QUESTION:

How do I deal with the hardships and struggles of life?

🗝 KEY IDEA:

I can deal with the hardships of life because of the hope I have in Jesus.

🗝 KEY VERSE:

Our hope is certain. It is something for the soul to hold on to. It is strong and secure. It goes all the way into the Most Holy Room behind the curtain. That is where Jesus has gone. He went there to open the way ahead of us.

Hebrews 6:19–20a

THINK ABOUT IT

When we have hope, we believe things will turn out well. It is natural to want to have hope. However, when we put our hope in things other than God, we will be disappointed eventually. Our key verse says our hope is certain, but it is only hope placed in God that is certain. When we hope in God's promises, we can count on those promises being kept, and that gives us renewed energy to keep going and stay faithful.

When Hope Doesn't Work

It's good to be hopeful, but it doesn't help to be hopeful if we are depending on something undependable. For instance, if we are hoping to be secure and happy, and we are depending on money to fulfill that hope, we will be let down because money can come and go.

Command people who are rich in this world not to be proud. Tell them not to put their hope in riches. Wealth is so uncertain. Command those who are rich to put their hope in God. He richly provides us with everything to enjoy.   1 TIMOTHY 6:17

If we are hoping to be kept safe from danger and we are depending on people to protect us, they will not be enough. God is more powerful than people.

> It is better to go to the LORD for safety
>   than to trust in mere human beings.
> **It is better to go to the LORD for safety**
>   **than to trust in human leaders.**   PSALM 118:8–9

If we are hoping for guidance and direction and we are relying on idols, which are replacements for God we make ourselves, we will be disappointed. Anything we rely on more than God is a poor substitute—it cannot speak to us as God can.

"If someone carves a statue of a god, what is it worth?
    What value is there in a god
    that teaches lies?
The one who trusts in this kind of god
    worships his own creation.
    He makes statues of gods that can't speak.
How terrible it will be for the Babylonians!
    They say to a wooden god, 'Come to life!'
They say to a stone god, 'Wake up!'
    Can those gods give advice?
They are covered with gold and silver.
    They can't even breathe."   HABAKKUK 2:18–19

Hope in God Gives Us Strength

If anyone ever needed hope, it was the people of Judah in the Old Testament. They were facing many years of captivity in Babylon, and they did not know what was going to happen to them. The prophet Isaiah was sent to encourage them with a message of comfort from God. Isaiah based his words of hope on the promises and power of God. When we place our hope in what God says and who God is, we will not be let down or disappointed. In fact, hope in God energizes us. What we hope for will happen—we can count on it!

The LORD and King is coming with power.
    He rules with a powerful arm.
He has set his people free.
    He is bringing them back as his reward.
    He has won the battle over their enemies.
He takes care of his flock like a shepherd.
    He gathers the lambs in his arms.
He carries them close to his heart.
    He gently leads those that have little ones.   ISAIAH 40:10–11

"So who will you compare me with?
    Who is equal to me?" says the Holy One.
Look up toward the sky.
    Who created everything you see?

The LORD causes the stars to come out at night one
by one.
He calls out each one of them by name.
His power and strength are great.
So none of the stars is missing.

Family of Jacob, why do you complain,
"The LORD doesn't notice our condition"?
People of Israel, why do you say,
"Our God doesn't pay any attention to our rightful
claims"?
Don't you know who made everything?
Haven't you heard about him?
The LORD is the God who lives forever.
He created everything on earth.
He won't become worn out or get tired.
No one will ever know how great his understanding is.
He gives strength to those who are tired.
He gives power to those who are weak.
Even young people become worn out and get tired.
Even the best of them trip and fall.
But those who trust in the LORD
will receive new strength.
They will fly as high as eagles.
They will run and not get tired.
They will walk and not grow weak.　　　ISAIAH 40:25–31

Hope in God Keeps Us Faithful

It is a proven fact that people with hope outlive people who have lost their hope. When we have unshakeable hope that God will keep his promises, it keeps us going when others would have given up. That is why Simeon in the New Testament lived such a long and faithful life. The Holy Spirit had promised Simeon that he would one day see the Messiah (Jesus). Simeon waited patiently for this promise to come true, and even though he was elderly, his hope gave him strength to live and serve God each new day.

In Jerusalem there was a man named Simeon. He was a good and godly man. He was waiting for God's promise to Israel to come true. The Holy Spirit was with him. The Spirit had told Simeon that he would not die before he had seen the Lord's Messiah. The Spirit led him into the temple courtyard. Then Jesus' parents brought the child in. They came to do for him what the Law required. Simeon took Jesus in his arms and praised God. He said,

> "Lord, you are the King over all.
>> Now let me, your servant, go in peace.
>> That is what you promised.
> My eyes have seen your salvation.
>> You have prepared it in the sight of all nations.
> It is a light to be given to the Gentiles.
>> It will be the glory of your people Israel."

The child's father and mother were amazed at what was said about him. Then Simeon blessed them. He said to Mary, Jesus' mother, "This child is going to cause many people in Israel to fall and to rise. God has sent him. But many will speak against him. The thoughts of many hearts will be known. A sword will wound your own soul too."   LUKE 2:25–35

Discussion Questions:

1. Our key verse, Hebrews 16:19–20, says our hope is certain, which means we can count on it. Why is our hope so certain?

2. We learned that hope doesn't work when you hope in things like money, people or things that replace God. Have you ever put your hope in something other than God? If so, what?

3. The prophet Isaiah said that even young people become worn out and get tired and trip and fall. When has that happened to you? What does Isaiah say you should you do to get re-energized by the Lord?

Patience

🔑 **KEY QUESTION:**
How does God help me wait?

🔑 **KEY IDEA:**
I do not get angry quickly, and I am patient, even when things go wrong.

🔑 **KEY VERSE:**
Anyone who is patient has great understanding.
But anyone who gets angry quickly shows how foolish
they are. *Proverbs 14:29*

THINK ABOUT IT

Patience is what God builds in us when we have to wait for something we want very badly, or when we have to control our temper. Patience is one of the most difficult qualities for many people to develop, because when we want something, we want it now! It can also be hard not to get angry quickly, especially when somebody is irritating us. But God is very patient with us, so if we want to be like him, we need to wait on God's timing and not lose our temper.

Patience Is Waiting on God's Timing

When he was a young teenager, David was told he would become the next king of Israel. But he was not crowned king until he was thirty years old—more than fifteen years later. While David waited on God's timing, King Saul grew more and more jealous of David and his growing popularity and wanted to kill him. For much of the time he waited, David was forced to run and hide from Saul. David had opportunities to kill Saul, and he was urged to do so by his men who thought he ought to be made king right away. But David waited patiently for God to be the one to take care of things at the right time.

Saul returned from chasing the Philistines. Then he was told, "David is in the Desert of En Gedi." So Saul took 3,000 of the best soldiers from the whole nation of Israel. He started out to look for David and his men. He planned to look near the Rocky Cliffs of the Wild Goats.

He came to some sheep pens along the way. A cave was there. Saul went in to go to the toilet. David and his men were far back in the cave. David's men said, "This is the day the LORD told you about. He said to you, 'I will hand your enemy over to you. Then you can deal with him as you want to.'" So David came up close to Saul without being seen. He cut off a corner of Saul's robe.

Later, David felt sorry that he had cut off a corner of Saul's robe. He said to his men, "May the LORD keep me from doing a thing like that again to my master. He is the LORD's anointed

king. So I promise that I will never lay my hand on him. The LORD has anointed him." David said that to correct his men. He wanted them to know that they should never suggest harming the king. He didn't allow them to attack Saul. So Saul left the cave and went on his way.

Then David went out of the cave. He called out to Saul, "King Saul! My master!" When Saul looked behind him, David bowed down. He lay down flat with his face toward the ground. He said to Saul, "Why do you listen when men say, 'David is trying to harm you'? This day you have seen with your own eyes how the LORD handed you over to me in the cave. Some of my men begged me to kill you. But I didn't. I said, 'I will never lay my hand on my master. He is the LORD's anointed king.' Look, my father! Look at this piece of your robe in my hand! I cut off the corner of your robe. But I didn't kill you. See, there is nothing in my hand that shows I am guilty of doing anything wrong. I haven't turned against you. I haven't done anything to harm you. But you are hunting me down. You want to kill me. May the LORD judge between you and me. And may the LORD pay you back because of the wrong things you have done to me. But I won't do anything to hurt you. People say, 'Evil acts come from those who do evil.' So I won't do anything to hurt you.

"King Saul, who are you trying to catch? Who do you think you are chasing? I'm nothing but a dead dog or a flea! May the LORD be our judge. May he decide between us. May he consider my case and stand up for me. May he show that I'm not guilty of doing anything wrong. May he save me from you." 1 SAMUEL 24:1–15

Patience Is Waiting for an Answer to Prayer

David had to wait more than fifteen years for God to fulfill his promise. David was patient enough to wait for God's timing. It also takes patience to wait for answers to prayer. Sometimes we don't know why God takes so long to respond to our request, especially when we need help badly, such as when we are sick or hurt. Poor health can make life much harder. It can make it difficult to be patient and wait for God's answer to our prayer. When we don't feel well, we just want God to heal us immediately! But being patient pays off, as it did for the man at the pool.

Jesus went up to Jerusalem for one of the Jewish feasts. In Jerusalem near the Sheep Gate is a pool. In the Aramaic language it is called Bethesda. It is surrounded by five rows of columns with a roof over them. Here a great number of disabled people used to lie down. Among them were those who were blind, those who could not walk, and those who could hardly move. One person was there who had not been able to walk for 38 years. Jesus saw him lying there. He knew that the man had been in that condition for a long time. So he asked him, "Do you want to get well?"

"Sir," the disabled man replied, "I have no one to help me into the pool when an angel stirs up the water. I try to get in, but someone else always goes down ahead of me."

Then Jesus said to him, "Get up! Pick up your mat and walk." The man was healed right away. He picked up his mat and walked.

This happened on a Sabbath day. So the Jewish leaders said to the man who had been healed, "It is the Sabbath day. The law does not allow you to carry your mat."

But he replied, "The one who made me well said to me, 'Pick up your mat and walk.'"

They asked him, "Who is this fellow? Who told you to pick it up and walk?"

The one who was healed had no idea who it was. Jesus had slipped away into the crowd that was there.

Later Jesus found him at the temple. Jesus said to him, "See, you are well again. Stop sinning, or something worse may happen to you." The man went away. He told the Jewish leaders it was Jesus who had made him well.　　　　　　　　　　　　JOHN 5:1–15

Patience Is Not Losing Your Temper

Patience is what it takes to wait for something, but it is also what we need to help us get along with others. The opposite of a patient person is one who gets angry quickly, has a bad temper or fights with others. That doesn't sound like someone who wants to be like Jesus! Read the following verses to discover why it's good to be patient and why it's not so good to be impatient.

> Anyone who is patient has great understanding.
>   But anyone who gets angry quickly shows how foolish
>   they are.   PROVERBS 14:29

> A person with a bad temper stirs up conflict.
>   But a person who is patient calms things down.
>   PROVERBS 15:18

> It is better to be patient than to fight.
>   It is better to control your temper than to take a city.
>   PROVERBS 16:32

My dear brothers and sisters, pay attention to what I say. Everyone should be quick to listen. But they should be slow to speak. They should be slow to get angry. Human anger doesn't produce the holy life God wants.   JAMES 1:19–20

Discussion Questions:

1. In what areas of life do you struggle to have patience?

2. What is the longest time you have had to wait for something? What helped you to have patience?

3. Read the section entitled "Patience is Not Losing Your Temper" out loud, adjusting the words so you can put your name in every line. For example, "Justin is patient and has great understanding. But if Justin gets angry quickly it shows how foolish he is." Mark your favorite statement.

Kindness/Goodness

🔑 KEY QUESTION:

What does it mean to do the right thing?

🔑 KEY IDEA:

I choose to be kind and good in my relationships with others.

🔑 KEY VERSE:

Make sure that no one pays back one wrong act with another. Instead, always try to do what is good for each other and for everyone else.   *1 Thessalonians 5:15*

THINK ABOUT IT

Have you ever had the fun of surprising someone with an act of kindness? Doing something kind for a person is like giving them a gift. It is especially wonderful to show kindness to a person who does not deserve it or expect it. When we are kind, we are treating people the way God treats us.

David Is Kind to Jonathan's Son

Back in Chapter 21, we read about the remarkable friendship between Jonathan, the son of King Saul, and David, the future king of Israel. King Saul was jealous of David and wanted to kill him, but Jonathan risked his life to protect David. Before they parted ways for the last time, Jonathan asked David to make an important promise to him and his family:

"But always be kind to me, just as the LORD is. Be kind to me as long as I live. Then I won't be killed. And never stop being kind to my family. Don't stop even when the LORD has cut off every one of your enemies from the face of the earth."   1 SAMUEL 20:14–15

Many years later, after Saul and Jonathan had both died, David remembered his friend's request to never stop being kind to his family. The way David kept his promise is a remarkable story of kindness.

David asked, "Is anyone left from the royal house of Saul? If there is, I want to be kind to him because of Jonathan."

Ziba was a servant in Saul's family. David sent for him to come and see him. The king said to him, "Are you Ziba?"

"I'm ready to serve you," he replied.

The king asked, "Isn't there anyone still alive from the royal house of Saul? God has been very kind to me. I would like to be kind to that person in the same way."

Ziba answered the king, "A son of Jonathan is still living. Both of his feet were hurt so that he can't walk."

"Where is he?" the king asked.

Ziba answered, "He's in the town of Lo Debar. He's staying at the house of Makir, the son of Ammiel."

So King David had Mephibosheth brought from Makir's house in Lo Debar.

Mephibosheth came to David. He was the son of Jonathan, the son of Saul. Mephibosheth bowed down to David to show him respect.

David said, "Mephibosheth!"

"I'm ready to serve you," he replied.

"Don't be afraid," David told him. "You can be sure that I will be kind to you because of your father Jonathan. I'll give back to you all the land that belonged to your grandfather Saul. And I'll always provide what you need."

Mephibosheth bowed down to David. He said, "Who am I? Why should you pay attention to me? I'm nothing but a dead dog."

Then the king sent for Saul's servant Ziba. He said to him, "I'm giving your master's grandson everything that belonged to Saul and his family. You and your sons and your servants must farm the land for him. You must bring in the crops. Then he'll be taken care of. I'll always provide what he needs." Ziba had 15 sons and 20 servants.

Then Ziba said to the king, "I'll do anything you command me to do. You are my king and master." So David provided what Mephibosheth needed. He treated him like one of the king's sons.

Mephibosheth had a young son named Mika. All the members of Ziba's family became servants of Mephibosheth. Mephibosheth lived in Jerusalem. The king always provided what he needed. Both of his feet were hurt so that he could not walk.

2 SAMUEL 9:1–13

Will Philemon Be Kind?

In the New Testament, we read Paul's unusual letter to Philemon. Onesimus was Philemon's slave, but he ran away. Onesimus met the apostle Paul, who happened to be a friend of Philemon. Onesimus became a Christian and decided that it would be right to return to Philemon. So Paul wrote a letter to Philemon, asking him to be kind to Onesimus and treat him as a Christian brother, not as a runaway slave.

I, Paul, am writing this letter. I am a prisoner because of Christ Jesus. Our brother Timothy joins me in writing.

Philemon, we are sending you this letter. You are our dear friend. You work together with us.   PHILEMON 1

Because of the authority Christ has given me, I could be bold. I could order you to do what you should do anyway. But we love each other. And I would rather appeal to you on the basis of that love. I, Paul, am an old man. I am now also a prisoner because of Christ Jesus. I am an old man, and I'm in prison. This is how I make my appeal to you for my son Onesimus. He became a son to me while I was being held in chains. Before that, he was useless to you. But now he has become useful to you and to me.

I'm sending Onesimus back to you. All my love for him goes with him. I'm being held in chains because of the good news. So I would have liked to keep Onesimus with me. And he could take your place in helping me. But I didn't want to do anything unless you agreed. Any favor you do must be done because you want to do it, not because you have to. Onesimus was separated from you for a little while. Maybe that was so you could have him back forever. You could have him back not as a slave. Instead, he would be better than a slave. He would be a dear brother. He is very dear to me but even more dear to you. He is dear to you not only as another human being. He is also dear to you as a brother in the Lord.

Do you think of me as a believer who works together with you? Then welcome Onesimus as you would welcome me. Has he done anything wrong to you? Does he owe you anything? Then charge it to me. I'll pay it back. I, Paul, am writing this with my own hand. I won't even mention that you owe me your life. My brother, we both belong to the Lord. So I wish I could receive some benefit from you. Renew my heart. We know that Christ is the one who really renews it. I'm sure you will obey. So I'm writing to you. I know you will do even more than I ask.   PHILEMON 8–21

How to Show Kindness

One day a well-known Jewish religious leader invited Jesus to a fancy dinner party. Only important people were invited

to such an event, and they carefully chose the best seats for themselves. Jesus used the opportunity to teach them about kindness.

Jesus noticed how the guests picked the places of honor at the table. So he told them a story. He said, "Suppose someone invites you to a wedding feast. Do not take the place of honor. A person more important than you may have been invited. If so, the host who invited both of you will come to you. He will say, 'Give this person your seat.' Then you will be filled with shame. You will have to take the least important place. But when you are invited, take the lowest place. Then your host will come over to you. He will say, 'Friend, move up to a better place.' Then you will be honored in front of all the other guests. All those who lift themselves up will be made humble. And those who make themselves humble will be lifted up."

Then Jesus spoke to his host. "Suppose you give a lunch or a dinner," he said. "Do not invite your friends, your brothers or sisters, or your relatives, or your rich neighbors. If you do, they may invite you to eat with them. So you will be paid back. But when you give a banquet, invite those who are poor. Also invite those who can't see or walk. Then you will be blessed. Your guests can't pay you back. But you will be paid back when those who are right with God rise from the dead."   LUKE 14:7–14

Discussion Questions:

1. Share about a time when someone was kind to you.

2. Interestingly, the story Jesus told to encourage kindness is exactly what David did for Mephibosheth. Can you think of a way to include someone in your activities who is usually left out?

3. If you were giving advice to Philemon, how could you use our key verse, 1 Thessalonians 5:15, to encourage Philemon to be kind?

Faithfulness

🗝 **KEY QUESTION:**

Why is it important to be loyal and committed to God and others?

🗝 **KEY IDEA:**

I can be trusted because I keep my promises to God and others.

🗝 **KEY VERSE:**

Don't let love and truth ever leave you.
Tie them around your neck.
Write them on the tablet of your heart.
Then you will find favor and a good name
in the eyes of God and people.   *Proverbs 3:3–4*

THINK ABOUT IT

Why do we call dogs "man's best friend?" Because dogs are faithful to their owners. There are many stories of dogs who run happily to greet their master no matter how they were treated that morning, or dogs who won't leave the side of their sick owner, or dogs who defend a child from a wild animal, or dogs who find their way home when they're lost. We can learn a lot about faithfulness from our dogs. When we are loyal, when we keep our promises, and when we can be depended on, we are acting like our God!

Joseph: An Example of Faithfulness

We can learn a lot about faithfulness from the Old Testament story of Joseph. He was his father's obvious favorite, and his ten older brothers were jealous of him. When he was seventeen years old, he dreamt they would all bow down to him, which made them hate him even more. One day, he went to care for his brothers as they worked in the pastures. As they saw Joseph approach, wearing the special robe his father had given him, his brothers plotted to kill him. They changed their minds and decided to get money for him instead, and they sold him to some passing traders. But now, they had to make up a story to tell their father about his beloved son.

They got Joseph's beautiful robe. They killed a goat and dipped the robe in the blood. They took the robe back to their father. They said, "We found this. Take a look at it. See if it's your son's robe."

Jacob recognized it. He said, "It's my son's robe! A wild animal has eaten him up. Joseph must have been torn to pieces."

Jacob tore his clothes. He put on the rough clothing people wear when they're sad. Then he mourned for his son many days.

GENESIS 37:31–34

The traders sold Joseph to an Egyptian official to work as his slave. Some teenagers would have been so angry at such unfair treatment they would have hidden in their room and refused to work. But not Joseph. He was a faithful servant right from the start.

The LORD was with Joseph. He gave him great success. Joseph lived in Potiphar's house. Joseph's master saw that the LORD was with him. He saw that the LORD made Joseph successful in everything he did. So Potiphar was pleased with Joseph and made him his attendant. He put Joseph in charge of his house. He trusted Joseph to take care of everything he owned. From that time on, the LORD blessed Potiphar's family and servants because of Joseph. He blessed everything Potiphar had in his house and field. So Joseph took good care of everything Potiphar owned. With Joseph in charge, Potiphar didn't have to worry about anything except the food he ate. GENESIS 39:2–6A

Things were going well for Joseph. Then Potiphar's wife told Potiphar a lie about Joseph, and Joseph was thrown into prison where he was forgotten and left for years. Even though this was unjust, Joseph stayed faithful to God.

One night Pharaoh (the king of Egypt) had a dream that none of his wise men could interpret. Pharaoh heard about Joseph, the prisoner whose God told people the meanings of their dreams, and he called for him. Joseph told Pharaoh his dream was God's warning that there would be seven years of plenty, when a lot of food would grow in Egypt, followed by seven years of famine, when terrible hunger would destroy the land. He told Pharaoh to look for a wise man to put in charge of gathering the extra food during the seven years of plenty and distributing the stored food when the years of famine came. That way, the land of Egypt would be saved from destruction. Guess who Pharaoh chose as his wise man?

The plan seemed good to Pharaoh and all his officials. So Pharaoh said to them, "The spirit of God is in this man. We can't find anyone else like him, can we?"

Then Pharaoh said to Joseph, "God has made all this known to you. No one is as wise and understanding as you are. You will be in charge of my palace. All my people must obey your orders. I will be greater than you only because I'm the one who sits on the throne."

So Pharaoh said to Joseph, "I'm putting you in charge of the whole land of Egypt." Then Pharaoh took from his finger the ring he used to give his official stamp. He put it on Joseph's finger. He dressed him in robes made out of fine linen. He put a gold chain around Joseph's neck. He also had him ride in a chariot. Joseph was now next in command after Pharaoh. People went in front of Joseph and shouted, "Get down on your knees!" By doing all these things, Pharaoh put Joseph in charge of the whole land of Egypt.

GENESIS 41:37–43

As Joseph had predicted, there were seven years of good crops. Joseph made sure Egypt set aside food for the future famine. Although he was now a rich man, he stayed faithful to his promise to help the people of Egypt. When famine struck, Egypt was the only nation that was prepared. Meanwhile, back in Canaan where they were out of food, Joseph's father Jacob sent the ten brothers to Egypt. Joseph's dream was about to come true.

Jacob found out that there was grain in Egypt. So he said to his sons, "Why do you just keep looking at one another?" He continued, "I've heard there's grain in Egypt. Go down there. Buy some for us. Then we'll live and not die."

So ten of Joseph's brothers went down to Egypt to buy grain there.   GENESIS 42:1–3

Joseph was the governor of the land. He was the one who sold grain to all its people. When Joseph's brothers arrived, they bowed down to him with their faces to the ground.   GENESIS 42:6

Twenty-one years had gone by since Joseph dreamed about his brothers bowing to him. Joseph stayed faithful to God that whole time, even though his problems were worse than most. And God stayed faithful to Joseph. Because of this faithfulness, Joseph was able to save his family and his nation from the famine.

Mary: Another Example of Faithfulness

In the New Testament, God chose a faithful girl for an assignment that would lead to a blessing for the whole world. Young Mary got quite a shock when an angel appeared to tell her she would be the mother of God's Son. But her response shows us her heart of faithfulness.

God sent the angel Gabriel to Nazareth, a town in Galilee. He was sent to a virgin. The girl was engaged to a man named Joseph. He came from the family line of David. The virgin's name was Mary. The angel greeted her and said, "The Lord has blessed you in a special way. He is with you."

Mary was very upset because of his words. She wondered what kind of greeting this could be. But the angel said to her, "Do not be afraid, Mary. God is very pleased with you. You will become pregnant and give birth to a son. You must call him Jesus. He will be great and will be called the Son of the Most High God. The Lord God will make him a king like his father David of long ago. The Son of the Most High God will rule forever over his people. They are from the family line of Jacob. That kingdom will never end."

"How can this happen?" Mary asked the angel. "I am a virgin."

The angel answered, "The Holy Spirit will come to you. The power of the Most High God will cover you. So the holy one that is born will be called the Son of God." Luke 1:26b–35

"I serve the Lord," Mary answered. "May it happen to me just as you said it would." Then the angel left her. Luke 1:38

Discussion Questions:

1. What does our key verse, Proverbs 3:3–4, tell us to do? How does that help us to be faithful?

2. Joseph stayed faithful when his brothers rejected him, when he was punished for something he did not do, and even when he was rich and in charge of the whole land. During which of these times do you think it was hardest for Joseph to stay faithful?

3. A faithful person keeps promises, is loyal to friends, and can be trusted. What area of faithfulness do you need to work on?

29

Gentleness

🔑 **KEY QUESTION:**
How do I show thoughtfulness and consideration?

🔑 **KEY IDEA:**
I am thoughtful, considerate and calm with others.

🔑 **KEY VERSE:**
Let everyone know how gentle you are. The Lord is
coming soon.   *Philippians 4:5*

THINK ABOUT IT

*One time when Jesus was describing himself, he said, "I am
gentle." Some people would think he was calling himself a
weakling! But as we will see in this chapter, sometimes it takes
courage to be gentle. Gentleness helps angry people calm
down. A gentle person is thoughtful and considerate of the
needs of others. And it takes a gentle spirit to restore broken
relationships.*

Gentleness Saves the Day

*We find an example of gentleness in the Old Testament story
where David encounters Nabal and Abigail, a husband who
was cruel and his wife who was wise. David, before he was king,
spent years running and hiding from King Saul, who wanted to
kill him. While he was on the run, David got food and supplies
for his men as payment for protecting people's flocks, including
flocks belonging to Nabal. David and his men had done a good
job keeping Nabal's flocks safe, but when David's men asked
Nabal for some food, they got a cruel answer.*

Nabal answered David's servants, "Who is this David? Who is this son of Jesse? Many servants are running away from their masters these days. Why should I give away my bread and water? Why should I give away the meat I've prepared for those who clip the wool off my sheep? Why should I give food to men who come from who knows where?"

So David's men turned around and went back. When they arrived, they reported to David every word Nabal had spoken. David said to his men, "Each of you put on your swords!" So they did. David put his sword on too. About 400 men went up with David. Two hundred men stayed behind with the supplies.

1 SAMUEL 25:10–13

David was angry! He was determined to get revenge on Nabal. He was marching towards Nabal's home.

One of the servants warned Abigail, Nabal's wife. He said, "David sent some messengers from the desert to give his greetings to our master. But Nabal shouted at them and was rude to them. David's men had been very good to us. They treated us well. The whole time we were near them out in the fields, nothing was stolen. We were taking care of our sheep near them. During that time, they were like a wall around us night and day. They kept us safe. Now think it over. See what you can do. Horrible trouble will soon come to our master and his whole family. He's such an evil man that no one can even talk to him."

Abigail didn't waste any time. She got 200 loaves of bread and two bottles of wine. The bottles were made out of animal skins. She got five sheep that were ready to be cooked. She got a bushel of grain that had been cooked. She got 100 raisin cakes. And she got 200 cakes of pressed figs. She loaded all of it on the backs of donkeys. Then she told her servants, "Go on ahead. I'll follow you." But she didn't tell her husband Nabal about it.   1 SAMUEL 25:14–19

One of the most dramatic meetings in the Bible was about to take place. An angry David with 400 of his men were out to get revenge, and Abigail, loaded down with food, ran to intercept him. Read how Abigail gently convinced David not to sin.

When Abigail saw David, she quickly got off her donkey. She bowed down in front of David with her face toward the ground. She fell at his feet. She said, "Pardon your servant, sir. Please let me speak to you. Listen to what I'm saying. Let me take the blame myself. Please don't pay any attention to that evil man Nabal. His name means Foolish Person. And that's exactly what he is. He's always doing foolish things. I'm sorry I didn't get a chance to see the men you sent. Sir, the LORD has kept you from killing Nabal and his men. He has kept you from using your own hands to get even. So may what's about to happen to Nabal happen to all your enemies. May it happen to everyone who wants to harm you. And may it happen just as surely as the LORD your God and you are alive. I've brought a gift for you. Give it to the men who follow you."   1 SAMUEL 25:23–27

> *If Abigail had met David with force and anger, David could have gotten even madder and may have even killed Abigail on the spot. But Abigail saved the day by calming David down with her gentle approach. She was an example of the proverb that says, "A gentle answer turns anger away. But mean words stir up anger" (Proverbs 15:1).*

David said to Abigail, "Give praise to the LORD. He is the God of Israel. He has sent you today to find me. May the LORD bless you for what you have done. You have shown a lot of good sense. You have kept me from killing Nabal and his men this day. You have kept me from using my own hands to get even. It's a good thing you came quickly to meet me. If you hadn't come, not one of Nabal's men would have been left alive by sunrise. And that's just as sure as the LORD, the God of Israel, is alive. He has kept me from harming you."

Then David accepted from her what she had brought him. He said, "Go home in peace. I've heard your words. I'll do what you have asked."   1 SAMUEL 25:32–35

Gentleness Repairs a Friendship

In the New Testament, we see Jesus being gentle with people on many occasions. One time it was his disciple Peter who needed Jesus' gentleness. Peter had not been a faithful friend to Jesus. When Jesus was about to be killed, Peter told the people nearby that he did not know Jesus. In fact, he said it three times! Jesus had predicted Peter would fail him in this way, but Peter did not believe he could do such a terrible thing.

Now, in the days after Jesus rose from the dead and had been appearing to the disciples, Peter was still feeling badly about letting Jesus down. Peter and the others were out fishing when Jesus appeared again. With a heart of gentleness, Jesus spoke with Peter and gave him a chance to repair their friend-ship. Jesus even trusted Peter with a special responsibility to lead God's people.

Early in the morning, Jesus stood on the shore. But the disciples did not realize that it was Jesus.

He called out to them, "Friends, don't you have any fish?"

"No," they answered.

He said, "Throw your net on the right side of the boat. There you will find some fish." When they did, they could not pull the net into the boat. There were too many fish in it.

Then the disciple Jesus loved said to Simon Peter, "It is the Lord!" As soon as Peter heard that, he put his coat on. He had taken it off earlier. Then he jumped into the water. The other disciples followed in the boat. They were towing the net full of fish. The shore was only about 100 yards away. When they landed, they saw a fire of burning coals. There were fish on it. There was also some bread. John 21:4–9

When Jesus and the disciples had finished eating, Jesus spoke to Simon Peter. He asked, "Simon, son of John, do you love me more than these others do?"

"Yes, Lord," he answered. "You know that I love you."

Jesus said, "Feed my lambs."

Again Jesus asked, "Simon, son of John, do you love me?"

He answered, "Yes, Lord. You know that I love you."

Jesus said, "Take care of my sheep."

Jesus spoke to him a third time. He asked, "Simon, son of John, do you love me?"

Peter felt bad because Jesus asked him the third time, "Do you love me?" He answered, "Lord, you know all things. You know that I love you."

Jesus said, "Feed my sheep." John 21:15–17

Peter's relationship with Jesus was gently restored. Jesus calls each of us to follow him with gentle words like these:

"Come to me, all you who are tired and are carrying heavy loads. I will give you rest. Become my servants and learn from me. I am gentle and free of pride. You will find rest for your souls. Serving me is easy, and my load is light." Matthew 11:28–30

Discussion Questions:

1. Our key verse, Philippians 4:5, tells us that everyone who knows us should be able to see gentleness in us. Is that true of you? How do you show gentleness?

2. Have you had an experience where gentleness helped someone calm down? Why does gentleness help?

3. When do you find you need someone to show you gentleness? How does it feel to receive gentleness when you need it most?

30

Humility

⚷ **KEY QUESTION:**
What does it mean to value others before myself?

⚷ **KEY IDEA:**
I choose to value others more than myself.

⚷ **KEY VERSE:**
Don't do anything only to get ahead. Don't do it because you are proud. Instead, be humble. Value others more than yourselves. None of you should look out just for your own good. Each of you should also look out for the good of others. *Philippians 2:3–4*

THINK ABOUT IT

Humility is thinking rightly about who we are in comparison to God and others. Pride is thinking wrongly about who we are in comparison to God and others. Humility says, "God is God and I am not." Pride says, "I can do God's job." Humility says, "God gave me the ability to do this." Pride says, "I did this myself." Humility says, "You first." Pride says, "Me first." Which kind of person do you prefer to be around? Which kind of person do you want to be?

God Sometimes Helps Us Learn Humility

King Nebuchadnezzar in the Old Testament learned a hard lesson about being humble. He had a dream about a large tree that was cut down to its stump. Then in his dream a heavenly messenger predicted the king would live outside with the wild animals for seven periods of time. When Daniel heard the dream, it terrified him. He reluctantly told the king what his dream meant. It was God's warning about what would happen to King Nebuchadnezzar if he did not change his ways. When the king showed pride by taking credit for the blessings that God had given him, his terrifying dream immediately came true.

"Your Majesty, here is what your dream means. The Most High God has given an order against you. You will be driven away from people. You will live with the wild animals. You will eat grass just as an ox does. You will become wet with the dew of heaven. Seven periods of time will pass by for you. Then you will recognize that the Most High God rules over all kingdoms on earth. He gives them to anyone he wants. But he gave a command to leave the stump of the tree along with its roots. That means your kingdom will be given back to you. It will happen when you recognize that the God of heaven rules. So, Your Majesty, I hope you will accept my advice. Stop being sinful. Do what is right. Give up your evil practices. Show kindness to those who are being treated badly. Then perhaps things will continue to go well with you."

All this happened to King Nebuchadnezzar. It took place twelve months later. He was walking on the roof of his palace in Babylon. He said, "Isn't this the great Babylon I have built as a place for my royal palace? I used my mighty power to build it. It shows how glorious my majesty is."

He was still speaking when he heard a voice from heaven. It said, "King Nebuchadnezzar, here is what has been ordered concerning you. Your royal authority has been taken from you. You will be driven away from people. You will live with the wild animals. You will eat grass just as an ox does. Seven periods of time will pass by for you. Then you will recognize that the Most High God rules over all kingdoms on earth. He gives them to anyone he wants."

What had been said about King Nebuchadnezzar came true at once. He was driven away from people. He ate grass just as an ox does. His body became wet with the dew of heaven. He stayed that way until his hair grew like the feathers of an eagle. His nails became like the claws of a bird.

At the end of that time I, Nebuchadnezzar, looked up toward heaven. My mind became clear again. Then I praised the Most High God. I gave honor and glory to the God who lives forever.

> His rule will last forever.
>   His kingdom will never end.
> He considers all the nations on earth
>   to be nothing.
> He does as he pleases
>   with the powers of heaven.
> He does what he wants
>   with the nations of the earth.
> No one can hold back his hand.
>   No one can say to him,
>   "What have you done?"

My honor and glory were returned to me when my mind became clear again. The glory of my kingdom was given back to me. My advisers and nobles came to me. And I was put back on my throne. I became even greater than I had been before. Now

I, Nebuchadnezzar, give praise and honor and glory to the King of heaven. Everything he does is right. All his ways are fair. He is able to bring down those who live proudly.   DANIEL 4:24–37

Jesus: The Perfect Example

Humility is an important part of living for Jesus. People who possess humility know that they are no more important than anyone else. Humble people put others' needs ahead of their own. The opposite of humility is pride and arrogance. Jesus is history's best example of humility. The God of the universe could have worn fancy clothing and ridden into our world on a white horse. Instead he came in the form of a helpless baby who was born to poor parents and placed in a dirty manger. Not long before Jesus died, he demonstrated humility to his disciples. He then instructed them to show humility to one another.

It was just before the Passover Feast. Jesus knew that the time had come for him to leave this world. It was time for him to go to the Father. Jesus loved his disciples who were in the world. So he now loved them to the very end.

They were having their evening meal. The devil had already tempted Judas, son of Simon Iscariot. He had urged Judas to hand Jesus over to his enemies. Jesus knew that the Father had put everything under his power. He also knew he had come from God and was returning to God. So he got up from the meal and took off his outer clothes. He wrapped a towel around his waist. After that, he poured water into a large bowl. Then he began to wash his disciples' feet. He dried them with the towel that was wrapped around him.

He came to Simon Peter. "Lord," Peter said to him, "are you going to wash my feet?"

Jesus replied, "You don't realize now what I am doing. But later you will understand."

"No," said Peter. "You will never wash my feet."

Jesus answered, "Unless I wash you, you can't share life with me."

"Lord," Simon Peter replied, "not just my feet! Wash my hands and my head too!"

Jesus answered, "People who have had a bath need to wash only their feet. The rest of their body is clean. And you are clean. But not all of you are." Jesus knew who was going to hand him over to his enemies. That was why he said not every one was clean.

When Jesus finished washing their feet, he put on his clothes. Then he returned to his place. "Do you understand what I have done for you?" he asked them. "You call me 'Teacher' and 'Lord.' You are right. That is what I am. I, your Lord and Teacher, have washed your feet. So you also should wash one another's feet. I have given you an example. You should do as I have done for you. What I'm about to tell you is true. A slave is not more important than his master. And a messenger is not more important than the one who sends him. Now you know these things. So you will be blessed if you do them."

JOHN 13:1–17

Discussion Questions:

1. What was King Nebuchadnezzar's opinion about himself before his dream came true? What was his opinion about himself after his mind cleared?

2. Read the six sentences in our key verse, Philippians 2:3–4. What are the three things it says a humble person should not do? What are the things a humble person should do? Which of these things do you think you need to work on?

3. How could you show humility instead of pride while doing something you are good at?

Epilogue

Only eight years old when he became king, Josiah demonstrated that he followed his ancestor David — leading the people of Judah to walk again in faithfulness to the Lord. God is on the lookout for more kids like Josiah! God needs young people who believe in him and want to follow him. You know now what God wants you to believe, what he wants you to do, and who he wants you to become.

Do you believe in God?
Do you believe God loves you?
Do you believe God cares for you?
Are you willing to follow Jesus?
Will you trust and obey the Bible?

If your answer is yes to all these questions, then you are ready to join God in his good work in this world. What is his assignment for you?

God wants you to love those who are hurting.
God wants you to be patient with everyone.
God wants you to obey your parents and teachers.
God wants you to be gentle with people and animals.
God wants you to keep your promises.
God wants you to let others go first.
God wants you to share your things with others.
God wants you to be happy.
God wants you to help others smile more.
God wants you to be courageous when you face new and scary situations.

If you BELIEVE, then shout it out: "Yes, I BELIEVE!"

To be read by the parent or teacher:
Helping a young person through this adventure — whether you are a parent, grandparent, teacher, mentor, aunt or uncle — is a noble and worthy task from God. Congratulations and thank you for investing in one of God's precious little ones.

The journey doesn't end here. This young person still has a great deal of growing to do. They will need someone to walk beside them day by day, helping them learn to apply what they have read in this book. They will need someone to offer them grace when they fail or go backwards. They will need someone to cheer them on when they get it right.

May you and a group of other adults stand with this child through their journey with God. Continue to go over the key ideas and memory verses. Look for opportunities in the course of each day to reinforce what they've learned.

Believe is meant to be completed more than once. There are two editions for children (ages 4–8 and 8–12), a student edition (ages 13–18) and an adult edition. Readers can experience and learn about these core Christian beliefs, practices and virtues through each stage of their development.

Of course, nothing will have more impact on a child than watching you personally grow and apply these truths in your own life. The Christian life is as much "caught" as it is "taught." So, continue your own journey and adventure with God. Let the child you mentored through this journey know where you stand.

Shout out to them, "Yes, I BELIEVE too!"

List of Bible Excerpts

Chapter 1: God
Genesis 1:1–26
Luke 3:15–18
Luke 3:21–22

Chapter 2: Personal God
Psalm 23:1–6
Matthew 6:25–33
Romans 8:26–28
Romans 8:38–39

Chapter 3: Salvation
Genesis 2:8–9
Genesis 2:15–17
Genesis 3:1–6
Genesis 3:13
Matthew 27:45–54
Matthew 28:1–7
John 3:16

Chapter 4: The Bible
Exodus 3:1–8a
Exodus 3:10
Exodus 20:1–17
Matthew 4:1–11

Chapter 5: Identity in Christ
Genesis 17:1–7
Genesis 17:15–17
Genesis 21:1–6
John 1:12–13
Ephesians 1:4–5
Ephesians 2:19
Luke 19:1–9

Chapter 6: Church

Genesis 12:1–3
Genesis 15:5–6
Matthew 16:13–18a
Acts 1:4–5
Acts 1:8–9
Acts 2:1–8
Acts 2:36–41

Chapter 7: Humanity

Genesis 4:2b–16
John 3:16
John 3:36
John 4:14
John 5:24
John 6:37
John 6:51
John 8:12
John 8:51
Matthew 18:12–14

Chapter 8: Compassion

Ruth 2:1–13
Ruth 2:15–20
Luke 10:25–37

Chapter 9: Stewardship

Genesis 1:28–30
1 Samuel 1:9–20
1 Samuel 1:24–28
1 Samuel 2:18–21
Mark 12:41–44

Chapter 10: Eternity

2 Kings 2:7–18
John 14:1–3
Revelation 21:1–4
Revelation 21:18–27

Chapter 11: Worship

Daniel 6:10–24
Acts 16:22–35
1 Corinthians 11:23b–26

Chapter 12: Prayer

Matthew 26:36–46
Luke 11:1–4
Luke 11:9–10
Philippians 4:6
Judges 6:14–16
Judges 6:36–40
Judges 7:7–8a
Judges 7:17–22a

Chapter 13: Bible Study

Joshua 1:5–9
Psalm 119:9–11
Psalm 119:15–16
Psalm 119:18
Psalm 119:35–36
Psalm 119:105
Matthew 13:1–23

Chapter 14: Single-Mindedness

2 Chronicles 20:1
2 Chronicles 20:3–4
2 Chronicles 20:12
2 Chronicles 20:15
2 Chronicles 20:17–19
2 Chronicles 20:20–22a
2 Chronicles 20:23–26
2 Chronicles 20:27–30
Matthew 14:25–33

Chapter 15: Total Surrender

Daniel 3:16–28
Esther 4:8b–16
Acts 7:51–60

Chapter 16: Biblical Community

Nehemiah 2:11—3:2
Nehemiah 6:15
Acts 2:42–47
Acts 4:32–37
1 John 3:16-18

Chapter 17: Spiritual Gifts
Daniel 2:1–5
Daniel 2:25–28
Daniel 2:31–35
Daniel 2:45b–47
1 Corinthians 12:7–22

Chapter 18: Offering My Time
Jonah 1:1–5
Jonah 1:9–17
Jonah 2:10
Haggai 1:2–11
Luke 2:41–49

Chapter 19: Giving My Resources
Ecclesiastes 5:10–12
Ecclesiastes 5:15
Ecclesiastes 5:19
Exodus 35:21–29
Exodus 36:3–6
Matthew 2:1–5a
Matthew 2:7–12

Chapter 20: Sharing My Faith
Jonah 3:3–5a
Jonah 3:6–7a
Jonah 3:8–10
John 4:7–18
John 4:28–29
John 4:39–42
Acts 8:26–32
Acts 8:34–38

Chapter 21: Love
1 Samuel 18:1b–4
1 Samuel 19:1–6
1 Samuel 20:18–23
1 Samuel 20:30–42
John 10:11–18

Chapter 22: Joy

Luke 2:6–20
Nehemiah 8:2–3
Nehemiah 8:9–12
Nehemiah 8:16–17
James 1:2–5
Philippians 4:11b–13
1 Peter 1:6–9

Chapter 23: Peace

Genesis 13:5–9
Genesis 13:14–18
1 Kings 3:3–15
1 Kings 4:24–25
Mark 4:35–41

Chapter 24: Self-Control

Judges 16:4–21
Judges 16:28–30
Luke 15:11–24

Chapter 25: Hope

1 Timothy 6:17
Psalm 118:8–9
Habakkuk 2:18–19
Isaiah 40:10–11
Isaiah 40:25–31
Luke 2:25–35

Chapter 26: Patience

1 Samuel 24:1–15
John 5:1–15
Proverbs 14:29
Proverbs 15:18
Proverbs 16:32
James 1:19–20

Chapter 27: Kindness/Goodness

1 Samuel 20:14–15
2 Samuel 9:1–13
Philemon 1
Philemon 8–21
Luke 14:7–14

Chapter 28: Faithfulness

Genesis 37:31–34
Genesis 39:2–6a
Genesis 41:37–43
Genesis 42:1–3
Genesis 42:6
Luke 1:26b–35
Luke 1:38

Chapter 29: Gentleness

1 Samuel 25:10–13
1 Samuel 25:14–19
1 Samuel 25:23–27
1 Samuel 25:32–35
John 21:4–9
John 21:15–17
Matthew 11:28–30

Chapter 30: Humility

Daniel 4:24–37
John 13:1–17

BELIEVE

POWERED BY ZONDERVAN

Dear Reader,

Notable researcher George Gallup Jr. summarized his findings on the state of American Christianity with this startling revelation: "Churches face no greater challenge…than overcoming biblical illiteracy, and the prospects for doing so are formidable because **the stark fact is, many Christians don't know what they believe or why.**"

The problem is not that people lack a hunger for God's Word. Research tells us that the number one thing people want from their church is for it to help them understand the Bible, and that Bible engagement is the number one catalyst for spiritual growth. Nothing else comes close.

This is why I am passionate about the book you're holding in your hands: *Believe*— a Bible engagement experience to anchor every member of your family in the key teachings of Scripture.

The *Believe* experience helps you answer three significant questions: Can you clearly articulate the essentials of the faith? Would your neighbors or coworkers identify you as a Christian based on their interactions with you and your family? Is the kingdom of God expanding in your corner of the world?

Grounded in Scripture, *Believe* is a spiritual growth experience for all ages, taking each person on a journey toward becoming more like Jesus in their beliefs, actions, and character. There is one edition for adults, one for students, and two versions for children. All four age-appropriate editions of *Believe* unpack the 10 key beliefs, 10 key practices, and 10 key virtues of a Christian, so that everyone in your family and your church can learn together to be more like Jesus.

When these timeless truths are understood, believed in the heart, and applied to our daily living, they will transform a life, a family, a church, a city, a nation, and even our world.

Imagine thousands of churches and hundreds of thousands of individuals all over the world who will finally be able to declare—**"I know what I believe and why, and in God's strength I will seek to live it out all the days of my life."** It could change the world. It has in the past; it could happen again.

In Him,

Randy Frazee
General Editor, *Believe*

LIVING THE STORY OF THE BIBLE TO BECOME LIKE JESUS

Teach your whole family how to live the story of the Bible!

- **Adults** – Unlocks the 10 key beliefs, 10 key practices, and 10 key virtues that help people live the story of the Bible. Bible Study DVD and Study Guide also available.
- *Think, Act, Be Like Jesus* – A companion to *Believe*, this fresh resource by pastor Randy Frazee will help readers develop a personal vision for spiritual growth and a simple plan for getting started on the *Believe* journey.
- **Students** – This edition contains fewer Scriptures than the adult edition, but with transitions and fun features to engage teens and students. Bible Study DVD also available.
- **Children** – With a Kids' Edition for ages 8-12, a Storybook for ages 4-8, a coloring book for toddlers, and four levels of curriculum for toddlers, preschool, early elementary, and later elementary, children of all ages will learn how to think, act, and be like Jesus.
- **Churches** – *Believe* is flexible, affordable, and easy to use with your whole church.
- **Spanish** – All *Believe* resources are also available in Spanish.

FOR ADULTS

9780310443834   9780310250173

FOR STUDENTS

9780310745617

FOR CHILDREN

Ages 8–12
9780310746010

Ages 4–8
9780310745907

Ages 2–5
9780310752226

FOR CHURCHES

Campaign Kit 9780310681717

BelieveTheStory.com

BELIEVE

POWERED BY ZONDERVAN

THE STORY

POWERED BY **ZONDERVAN®**

READ THE STORY. EXPERIENCE THE BIBLE.

Here I am, 50 years old. I have been to college, seminary, engaged in ministry my whole life, my dad is in ministry, my grandfather was in ministry, and **The Story has been one of the most unique experiences of my life.** The Bible has been made fresh for me. It has made God's redemptive plan come alive for me once again.
—Seth Buckley, Youth Pastor, Spartanburg Baptist Church, Spartanburg, SC

As my family and I went through *The Story* together, the more I began to believe and the more real [the Bible] became to me, and **it rubbed off on my children and helped them with their walk with the Lord.** *The Story* inspired conversations we might not normally have had.
—Kelly Leonard, Parent, Shepherd of the Hills Christian Church, Porter Ranch, CA

We have people reading *The Story*—**some devour it and can't wait for the next week.** Some have never really read the Bible much, so it's exciting to see a lot of adults reading the Word of God for the first time. I've heard wonderful things from people who are long-time readers of Scripture. They're excited about how it's all being tied together for them. It just seems to make more sense.
—Lynnette Schulz, Director of Worship Peace Lutheran Church, Eau Claire, WI

FOR ADULTS	FOR TEENS	FOR KIDS

	Ages 13+	Ages 8–12
9780310950974	9780310722809	9780310719250

Dive into the Bible in a whole new way!

The Story is changing lives, making it easy for any person, regardless of age or biblical literacy level, to understand the Bible.

The Story comes in five editions, one for each age group from toddlers to adults. All five editions are organized chronologically into 31 chapters with selected Scripture from Genesis to Revelation. The additional resources create an engaging group Bible-reading experience, whether you read *The Story* with your whole church, in small groups, or with your family.

- **Adults** – Read the Bible as one compelling story, from Genesis to Revelation. Available in NIV, KJV, NKJV, large print, imitation leather, and audio editions. Curriculum DVD and Participant's Guide also available.
- **Teens** – Teen edition of *The Story*, with special study helps and features designed with teens in mind. Curriculum DVD also available.
- **Children** – With a Kids' Edition for ages 8-12, a Storybook Bible for ages 4-8, a Storybook Bible for toddlers, fun trading cards, and three levels of curriculum for preschool, early elementary, and later elementary, children of all ages will learn how their story fits into God's story.
- **Churches** – *The Story* is flexible, affordable, and easy to use with your church, in any ministry, from nursery to adult Sunday school, small groups to youth group...and even the whole church.
- **Spanish** – *The Story* resources are also available in Spanish.

FOR CHILDREN

Ages 4–8
9780310719755

Ages 2–5
9780310719274

FOR CHURCHES

Campaign Kit   9780310941538

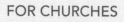

THE STORY
POWERED BY ZONDERVAN